LEGION OF THE WHITE TIGER

LEGION OF THE WHITE TIGER

James Watson

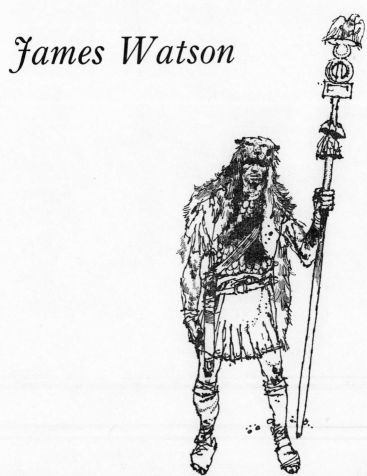

VICTOR GOLLANCZ LTD · LONDON
1973

ISBN 0 575 01728 7

MADE AND PRINTED IN GREAT BRITAIN BY
THE GARDEN CITY PRESS LIMITED
LETCHWORTH, HERTFORDSHIRE
SG6 1JS

For
Rosalind, Miranda and Francesca

Contents

An Historical Note

In the year 53 BC, Rome suffered one of the most crushing and humiliating military defeats in her history. It was at Carrhae in Syria. Ignoring the advice of his lieutenants and heedless of auguries of disaster, Marcus Crassus led 40,000 troops against the Parthians who were headed by a brilliant and treacherous young general, Surena.

Plutarch, in his life of Crassus, states that Surena "had concealed his main force behind the advance guard, and to prevent their being discovered by the glittering of their armour, he had ordered them to cover it with their coats or with skins".

Then the field "resounded with a horrid din and dreadful bellowing . . . While the Romans were trembling at the horrid noise, the Parthians suddenly uncovered their arms, and appeared like battalions of fire . . ." Plutarch goes on to give a most vivid description of the wretchedness of the Roman troops in the face of the swift-shooting Parthian archers.

Crassus' son, Publius, was cut down and beheaded. Crassus himself was killed and his head despatched to the Parthian King Orotes. Over 20,000 Romans lay dead. Some survivors escaped, but perhaps the most unfortunate—for the Parthians were a cruel, tyrannical people—were the 10,000 Romans who were taken into captivity. They played no further part in history, yet it is possible they did not all die in chains.

J. W.

I

Raft in the mist

There had been something. Through the thick mist that had lasted all day, a shape, suddenly clear on the slow swell of the waves, then gone. Cerdic ignored the rattle of spoon in pot from the deckhouse. Supper could wait. It would only be stew, and fat Silenos would have forgotten to salt it again.

Holding the rope lashings with one arm, Cerdic lowered himself till his feet skimmed the water. He crouched. Yes, there it was, rising and sinking, sea-washed. He sprang back on to the deck.

"Captain! Captain!"

He ran straight into the fleshy mountain of Silenos who had arrived with a dish of stew which now spilt over the deck. "Y' young bull! All that nourishment gone to waste, and me 'avin' remembered to put salt in it!"

Regardless of soup and nourishment, Cerdic sped on. "Captain, there's a wreck, an overturned boat—something out there!"

The ship's captain continued his meal as though he had not heard.

"We've got to save them. Please hurry!"

"In these waters," the captain replied, wiping his mouth on his sleeve, "we don't tarry even for the Goddess Diana. And pray keep your voice down or half the pirates in the Mediterranean will be on our tail."

Cerdic plunged away, to the two rowers at the stern of the Roman galley. "Turn her round!" The seamen ignored him. "I beg you!" Cerdic went in among them, grabbing at the oars.

Stirred to fury, the captain followed. The flat of his hand burst over Cerdic's ear, and the boy spun across the wet deck. "You could do with learning some Roman obedience."

The captain was about to give more advice. But he paused. His manner changed. He turned and bowed respectfully to the tall man who had stepped from behind the deckhouse. "My apologies, Sir, but it's your boy again. Not content with worrying the crew with his endless questions on seamanship, he wants command of my galley. He'll not be ruled."

"Uncle Mago!" cried Cerdic. "They must stop the ship. I saw people. In the mist."

Mago was a man of middle age with a black beard that enveloped his face like an unruly scarf. There were dashes of grey in the beard and a ripple of it in the hair stretching back from his immense forehead. He was lean, as though in his youth he had grown too tall for his strength. But there was no hint of frailty. His eyes, though fast losing their sight, radiated a warmth and power that commanded faith in him. He was a man whom others followed.

They called him The Carthaginian. Behind his back, other names were popular: The Mad Explorer, because he attempted journeys to places that geographers claimed did not exist, and Blackbeard the Magician, because of his genius as an inventor.

He carried a seven-foot sapling staff which he had named Hannibal's Leg and which he always swore, though with a twinkle in his eye, had belonged to the great Carthaginian general himself and helped him in his famous traverse of the Alps.

"People in the mist, Cerdic? Was there any movement? Did they shout or wave?"

From the fore-deck came the voice of Thyrsis, employed as Mago's master of transport. "The lad's always imagining things. My advice is, ignore him."

Mago reached out his hand for Cerdic. "Come closer." He brushed the matted fair hair from Cerdic's eyes. Their heads almost touched. "I may be going blind, gentlemen, and a mist such as this is virtually all I can see on the brightest of days, but I can still spot the light of truth in this lad's expression. Reverse course, Captain."

"But the pirates, Sir!"

"Pirates? Isn't General Pompey supposed to have cleared the seas of pirates? This ship is in my commission, do as I ask."

Mago was obeyed.

As the galley swung round, Cerdic took his uncle's arm and together they leaned out over the ship's side. On Mago's instructions, torches were lit. They seemed to consume the mist, for the air began to clear a little.

"HELLOO!" bellowed Mago through cupped hands. "Anybody there?"

Except for the dull lap of wave against wave, and wave against ship, there was silence.

"It's another the boy's jokes," complained Thyrsis, sourly. "He's due for a hiding." A tense, resentful man, whose unhappy life had embittered him, he stalked away. "He gets too many favours."

"Stop yer grumblin'," said Silenos, who loved Cerdic. "We're supposed to be cockin' an ear, aren't we?"

Then Cerdic saw it again. "There, Uncle! Something flat."

13

Mago shook his head. "I can see nothing, alas." But he called out, "HELLOO! HELLOO!"

"It's a raft, Uncle. There are two people."

The ship's captain had also seen them and a couple of crew members were roped round their waists and lowered to the water.

Close now. Two bodies, motionless, lay on a pathetically unseaworthy raft made of barrels crossed with ship's timber.

"They're dead," announced the captain. Yet in answer, one of the victims' heads rolled sideways. No words came, only the blinking of exhausted eyes. "Haul them aboard!"

Mouths open, limbs asprawl, the bodies slithered on to the deck, one a stocky, thick-necked man, the other a youth with a freckled face and gingery hair. "There's a flicker of life in this one, and no more," said the captain, holding the man's head. "The boy's already on his voyage over the Styx."

Mago ordered the others aside. "Let me see." He knelt down with his ear to the youth's heart. "If it has only just stopped beating—"

"Throw him overboard," interrupted Thyrsis, "and let's be on our way."

"This one's a slave," said the captain, indicating an iron band round the man's neck. "By Neptune! We turn the ship round, risking attack by pirates, for a slave—whatever next?"

Mago's temper spit like a fire fed with fresh-cut branches. "We shall answer in heaven for keeping slaves on earth, Captain. I suggest you return to your duties in navigating this ship."

While he spoke, Mago had turned the youth on to his chest. Gently, he began to press the youth's back downwards and forwards. Water spurted from his mouth. "Now quickly!" With Cerdic's help, Mago levered the youth on to his back, he raised his head and shoulders from the deck so that the head was propped at an angle.

Then he astonished those standing round him. He opened the youth's mouth. He began to breath into it, at the same time closing the nostrils with a finger and thumb.

"Only the gods can breathe life into the dead," snapped the captain.

"Don't you be too sure," countered Silenos. "See! T' lad's chest's movin' already."

Mago paused. He put mouth to mouth again, and blew, strongly but gently.

The rhythm continued: blow, wait, blow, wait, until Mago rested on his haunches. His face expressed satisfaction. "Our young friend's voyage over the Styx has been delayed. He will live."

The slave was trying to lift himself up. Cerdic brought him wine-spirit which quickly revived him, for he was powerfully built, with arms as muscular as a wrestler's.

Blankets were wrapped round the youth, and both the sea's victims were carried into the deckhouse.

"Will they be wantin' any stew, Master?" enquired Silenos. "I'll 'ave it 'ot again in two shakes o' a goat's beard."

Mago smiled away the tension of the last few minutes. "Now that we've saved their lives, Silenos, do you wish us to poison them?"

Silenos knew how to take a joke, and he laughed. "Both of 'em's bin in a right ol' scramble—bruises an' cuts fro' snifter to stern."

Mago asked Cerdic to reach him his "Bag of Tricks", as he called it, in which he kept everything precious and everything useful. He took out ointment and bandages. "You can occupy

15

those busy hands of yours, my boy, and put into practice some of the things I've taught you. You're company doctor now!"

As Cerdic confidently and skilfully dressed an open wound on the slave's forearm, Mago asked, "Have you strength, friend, to tell us of your misfortune?"

The slave merely stared back, as if under a spell.

"He's too frightened and too shocked to speak," Mago decided. "We'll learn nothing till he is completely rested . . . Yes, Silenos, give him food, a little at a time. But none of your fatty tit-bits, or he'll choke. Above all, we must keep them warm."

Later, on the open deck, Cerdic squatted down beside his uncle who was writing up his Log of the journey so far. "There's something in the Roman's hand he just won't let go. It'd take a hammer and chisel to prise his fingers apart."

Mago closed his Log. He nodded thoughtfully. "Probably something as dear to him as the youth's own life. It's curious, my boy, what power the mind has over the body, even at the threshhold of death. I've heard tell of people who can drive nails through their hands and, by strength of will, feel no pain . . . You observed one thing, and I another: we shall hear no words of explanation from the slave's mouth—his tongue has been cut out."

With a shudder, Cerdic imagined a sharp knife across his own tongue. "Could it have been the pirates, Uncle?"

"No, for the raw edges are healed. He has been a dumb man for a year at the very least."

"Will we be taking them with us on our journey?"

"That is for them to decide, though we could do with assistance since the plague robbed us of half our expedition. Whatever happens, we cannot leave them penniless in Syria.

They would be in the slave galleys before you could say 'Hannibal's Leg'!"

After days of billowing mist, the sun returned in splendour. The sea sparkled. The sky was radiant blue. Everyone was in good spirits, for there was less than a week's sailing to port.

Cedric's job was to watch over the young Roman boy whose exposure to the cold sea had caused a fever which, for all Mago's medicines, refused to leave him. He had to be forcibly fed. Periods of delirium, of terrified shouts and meaningless gabble, were followed by deep sleep.

At this moment the Roman lay peacefully, soothed, perhaps, by Cedric's quiet music. Given to him by Mago, Cedric's harp was his one treasured possession. It was fashioned from dark-grained wood covered with mysterious lettering—some sort of picture writing. On each side of the sound-box was an exquisitely inlaid dragon of polished carnelian, breathing flames of white crystal.

As his fingers glided over the strings, Cedric was wondering what sense could be made of the Roman's outbursts, "Where, father? Where?" and "Wait, wait for me! Gaius is gone, gone!"

It was obvious that Gaius was the young Roman's brother, but he gave no hint as to the identity of his father or where he lived.

The music unlocked Cedric's own memory. He was remembering all the voyages he had been on with his Uncle Mago, the adventures, the hardships, the thrills, always followed by a welcome return to Mago's island home off the north African coast. They never stayed in peace and tranquillity for long. Mago was as restless as the sea. "I put down my anchor," he would say, "just long enough to record my experiences and tabulate my findings—then the voices come to haunt me again, summoning me to unknown lands."

This was to be Mago's last and greatest voyage. On the first page of his Log he had written: "At an incalculable distance across the continent of the East, and beyond the North Wind, there lies a civilisation whose splendour outshines that of Greece or Rome. Many tales of such a civilisation have been carried West by merchants who have traded with the Parthians, and seamen speak in awe of a land beyond the farthest reaches of navigation.

"In Rome, men of learning have scorned my theories and declared me a fool and a madman, yet in my own country, they have greater faith. Though Carthage has lost all her sea-power and, in the face of Roman might, fallen upon evil days, her governors have commissioned my venture. My discoveries will be to the glory of Carthage, and in her name will I choose death before failure . . ."

What lies ahead, Cerdic wondered? Snow-capped mountains so high they pierce the heavens, so cold they turn all living matter to solid ice? Deserts full of scorpions twice the size of a man? And beyond the North Wind, who knows? Perhaps none of the treasures they promise you in stories, but a mighty precipice that plunges into everlasting darkness.

Cerdic's attention was snatched back to the present by a pained cry from the young Roman. "No, no! Take *my* life, take mine!" His scream brought the slave rushing to his side. "Wait! We've gold—for gold you will spare . . . Oh Gaius!" The slave cradled the youth's head in his arms. Then:

"Tryphon! Help us!" The boy's eyes were open. He saw the slave bending tenderly over him. "Tryphon? The gods be praised! Are we safe? Was it just a nightmare?"

Mago had come forward. He bent low to the sick Roman.

"The worst is over, my young friend. You are safe and among those who will care for you."

"But the pirates? And Gaius, my brother?" His eyes swung from face to face. He tried to rise. Failing, he extended his clasped hand. His fingers opened to reveal a gold ring with a stone of onyx. "My brother . . . my brother and I, we offer a prize of gold, twenty hectares of land—our inheritance—to anyone . . ." He was weakening. "Anyone who will tell us where we might find . . . might find." The sunlight beat into his eyes and made him dizzy. "The owner of this ring." The onyx stone was engraved with the figures of a piper and a dancing dog.

"You must rest," advised Mago, who had bid Silenos bring a cup of hot wine, "and take this medicinal potion which, through the gentle powers of sleep, will restore you to health again."

Mago's words calmed the Roman. His presence filled the youth with trust. "You will find Gaius, doctor? If my father should ever hear . . . But I tried, I tried! They . . . cut, they cut him down." He closed his eyes to stifle the memory. "At my feet. No ceremony, Gaius, at your parting . . . Father! I shall find you, with faithful Tryphon, I'll . . ."

Mago had dissolved a sleeping potion in the hot wine. He pressed the cup to the Roman's lips. "What is your name, my friend?"

"Festus."

"And your father?"

"War, gone." The Roman's head slipped drowsily forward. "Lost, so long, so long ago." His hand folded once more on the onyx ring. He was asleep.

"At least we know our new friends' names," said Mago, standing up. "Tryphon, you saved your master's life, that is clear. You search for his lost father, that too is obvious, and have sorely lost one of your party already. Then tell me, by nodding or shaking your head, is Festus' father a soldier?"

Tryphon smiled and nodded.

"Pirates attacked your ship and Gaius was killed, yes? You have indicated that you were nine days on the open sea and that your ship had been travelling eastwards, but how long ago was it since the boys had seen their father?"

The slave no longer smiled. He sighed deeply. He raised his outstretched fingers: five years, ten years . . .

Mago gasped in amazement. "Sixteen years! Is that possible, my friend? You nod. Yet Festus himself is scarcely sixteen. You nod again. Then—" Mago leaned heavily on his staff. "You are saying that Festus' father has been missing for sixteen years, and only now his sons begin their search for him? No, I am mistaken."

Tryphon pointed at his own chest. Then he put a finger to his eyes. He looked east. He drew a shape in the air.

"I am no wiser," confessed Mago.

"I think I know, Uncle," said Cerdic. "Tryphon has seen Festus' father in the east." Tryphon confirmed this vigorously. "You were with their father, Tryphon—in the Roman army?"

The slave mimed a battle scene. A defeat. "Come on, Cerdic, my boy," urged Mago, "You seem to be the one who reads this silent language best."

"They are taken prisoner. Beaten. Their hands are in chains. Years pass—am I right, Tryphon?"

"But sixteen years!" repeated Mago. He tugged at his beard. "A battle, a defeat in the east, sixteen years ago . . . I have it!" Mago held up his hand to check Tryphon's mime. "Carrhae!"

In delight and relief, the slave struggled to force out words from his tongueless mouth, and almost choked.

"I've never heard mention of a battle of Carrhae, Uncle."

"Little wonder, for it was a catastrophe for the Romans. They have never been so badly defeated on the field of battle. But I have heard rumours that the Parthian victors, though they left mountains of Roman dead, took many prisoners."

Tryphon was nodding again, and he was miming, tugging something apart with his hands, stooping, slinking forward, glancing over his shoulder.

"Escaping!" guessed Cerdic. "But alone. With the ring in his hand. Westwards, to Rome—no?"

Suddenly Tryphon was grabbed by invisible hands, thrown one way, then another, dragged, struck, cast down. His hands were at his mouth, covering it, protecting it, but in vain. His head was wrenched up, eyes closed in agony.

The story progressed. He was seated and chained, feeling the whiplash on his back. "After cutting out your tongue, Tryphon, the Parthians put you to work in the galleys. For how many years?"

Tryphon shrugged. Four, five, he could not be sure. "And then you escaped once more, reaching Italy, where you told Festus and his brother that their father was not dead, that he was a prisoner of the Parthians?"

The bones of the mystery had been revealed. "But five years, Tryphon, five years as a prisoner of as cruel a race as ever trod the earth!" Mago rocked his head sadly. "What a desperate venture!" He gazed at the sleeping Roman. "He would not recognise his father even if he saw him, and yet he risks his life to find him. He has lost his brother. He has lost his ship—and who knows what lies before him?"

Mago's mood changed. "Yet I need no reminding that our own enterprise is, in many ways, equally desperate." He rested his hand on Tryphon's shoulder. "Our journey, my friend, lies east and east and east! To where all known maps end. You and your young master are welcome to join our caravan till you decide your destination departs from ours."

His eyes were on the iron ring around the slave's throat. "But on one condition, that the band of servility is removed from your neck. None but free men voyage with Mago the Carthaginian."

2

Encounter with Parthians

"For many days," wrote Mago in his Log, "we have travelled eastwards from the sea coast of Syria, and entered the desert region of south western Parthian. So far, we have been allowed free passage by this warrior people, for they believe us to be harmless merchants. We have hired camels, packhorses and fifteen carriers.

"The heat grows more intense each day, the landscape more barren. Fortunately for my nephew Cerdic, whose spirit needs excitement as much as his body requires food, he now has a companion to share these empty days: Festus is quite recovered from his sea ordeal. He is a proud Roman, though recent experiences seem to have robbed him of confidence in himself.

"Cerdic, on the contrary, strikes people—especially Thyrsis, my baggage-master—as having too much confidence. I predict that Festus and Cerdic will be both friends and competitors. Already they vie with one another as to who can pitch the javelin farthest or who can mount a camel more swiftly.

"If we have had little adventure so far, then at least we have had cause for laughter. The sight of our portly master of the stewpot, Silenos, endeavouring to mount and ride a camel, still brings tears to our eyes when we remember it. Thirty times he was propped up between the poor beast's humps and thirty times he tumbled into the sand, forwards, backwards and finally head over heels. He has chosen a mule to ride on, declaring that Mother Nature was sleeping when camels were put together!

"Nothing grows but tufted grasses and hawthorn. There is no shelter. Formations of jagged rock rise from shelves of red shale, eroded and split by a million years of heat and wind. Colours blaze in the sunlight—browns, ochres and gold. The desert air is hollow and still. The slightest sound shatters this stillness as a drop of icy water destroys a heated glass.

"Many mountains and many deserts lie between us and the Land Beyond the North Wind, but our immediate objective is the range of mountains due east of us, bluer than the sky and hewn into ravines as purple as a Roman's cloak. If our good fortune holds, we shall reach them within seven days."

"Sand and rock, rock and sand!" Cerdic murmured. Since sunrise there had been the unchanging prospect of a desert track vanishing into the distance. He was angry at Thyrsis for refusing to let him feed the animals. He had made faces at him and got a stinging slap on the ear.

Partly because he wished to break the monotony of the journey and partly because he knew Thyrsis would protest, Cerdic challenged Festus to a race. "Over that ridge where the rocks look like spears, then on to the track again—Carthage versus Rome!"

"No racing," commanded Thyrsis. "The camels are not playthings."

"They *like* racing," countered Cerdic.

"What do you know about what they like?"

"I can understand camel-talk. Mine whispered in my ear

this very morning. 'If I don't stretch my legs soon,' he said, 'they'll drop off!'"

"You talk nonsense, boy."

"*I* might, but the camels don't . . . If my camel's legs fall off, it'll be your fault, Thyrsis. See! One's beginning to shake loose already."

Thyrsis was about to reply angrily, but Mago leaned towards him. His whispered comment made Thyrsis relent. "Very well, the Master and I think it's good for young ones to have their heads once in a while."

"Oo-ok!" whooped Cerdic, using the cry he had learnt from the camel traders when they wished to spur their beasts into action.

"Oo-ok!" echoed Festus. "To the top. Last there washes the other's dirty clothes for a week. Oo-ok! Oo-ok!"

The camels lumbered upwards over the red, crackling shale. Cerdic led Festus into a narrow gully scattered with boulders. His camel did not stumble once. It gave a nasal bleat and crashed through a screen of hawthorn on to the open crown of the summit. The young Roman was not so lucky. His mount lost its footing and sent him sprawling straight into a prickly hawthorn.

"Stop your laughing, Carthaginian!" Festus yelled as Cerdic pulled him free. "This race isn't over yet."

"You might bleed to death," grinned Cerdic.

Festus thrust his friend away. "It takes more than prickles to beat a Roman." He remounted. "To those rocks that look like a man's bald head."

Breathless, they reached the winning point together; and they were laughing for the camels seemed to have entered the spirit of the race as eagerly as their riders. "Let's agree not to wash our dirty clothes at all," suggested Cerdic.

For a while the friends were silent as they gazed out at the misty yellow plain. "You know, Cerdic, whenever I think of Rome's defeat at Carrhae, I imagine a place like this. Burning hot, the legions sweltering in their armour . . . and my father!' He hissed through hard-closed teeth. "How the Romans disgraced themselves on that day!"

"I'd like to know what the Romans were doing out here anyway," replied Cerdic. "They're too greedy by half, always wanting to steal other people's lands."

This remark stung Festus. "Romans, steal? They are not thieves, but warriors who live nobly and die bravely. I beg you, if you are to remain my friend, do not poke fun at a Roman's pride."

Cerdic looked away. He felt he had got himself into too many quarrels lately. He was going to speak, apologise, but Festus forestalled him.

"Why are we exchanging hurtful words?" He lowered his head. "Who can be sure of anything? My bitterness pours from me like wine from a broken cup. I am not grave as a Roman should be. But my father—does he live? And if he lives, how does he live—a lame beggar drifting through the cities of Parthia, broken and changed?

"He is a ghost to me, for he left for Syria before I was born. We would not recognise each other, and yet I am sworn to spend my life searching for him."

Only now did Cerdic really begin to understand how heavily Festus' task bore upon him. One day he had been a carefree youth, enjoying the life of a well-to-do Roman; the next he carried the burden of his brother's death, the loss of their family fortunes and the daunting prospect of tracing one Roman prisoner among the thousands that the Parthians had enslaved.

Cerdic raised his hand in salute. "I suggest Carthage and Rome sign a peace treaty. First one to cackle like a silly goose gets a free kick up the—"

"Look!" Festus had stiffened, half turning away. He pointed towards a cluster of rocks to the east of the caravan's route. "Can you see them?"

"Horsemen!"

Festus dug his heels into his mount. The camel swayed forward. "They're going to attack the caravan . . . We must give the alarm."

The horsemen were being led out by a rider astride a white stallion. A purple cloak swung from his shoulders.

"Wait a moment," warned Cerdic. "Those aren't horse*men* at all—they're boys! Our own age, having some fun."

With loud hoots and yells the youthful horsemen charged towards the caravan, raising dust and clattering over broken stones. Cerdic and Festus descended after them, silently, back down the gully, and wheeling into the open.

"I don't think I like their idea of fun," said Festus. "They'll terrify the animals."

The caravan had halted. Camels bleated. Packhorses shied away. The horsemen rode between them as the teeth of a comb strike through hair. They cheered. They reined and came charging back. Their whips were out. The caravan's neat line was shattered and the frightened beasts were driven in all directions.

"Hold still everyone!" Mago commanded. "No arms, not a word!"

Thyrsis' broad-sword was half-drawn. Mago's stern glance was on him. Reluctantly he slid the blade back into its scabbard. Silenos' fingers reached for a long-handled pan. He removed them as a whip end bit him across the arm. His mule bucked and he nearly fell.

"They are boys," called Mago. "They will soon tire of their sport."

The camels bearing Cerdic and Festus came loping across the sand.

"Why don't they fight?" Festus wanted to know. "Has Mago's magic turned the caravan to statues?"

The young Parthians were equally as astonished. Their leader called off the attack. There was no joy in beating an enemy who refused to defend himself. He was curious. While his comrades remained in a circle round the caravan, he rode up to Mago. He was swarthy, olive-skinned, with long black hair falling over the purple cloak which he furled proudly over his shoulders.

His tunic and trousers, both billowing in the sharp breeze from the mountains, were of a shiny, luxurious material which none in the caravan had ever seen before. He spoke in the Roman tongue. "You will bow to the son of a prince, or the whips of my friends shall persuade you."

Mago did not hesitate. He smiled a little. He bowed slightly from the shoulders. "Greetings, son of a prince."

"My father owns all the land that your eyes can see—and you trespass upon it. You are Romans, the scum of the earth." The youth spat into the sand. "Scum! Not worthy to lick a Parthian shadow."

Festus would have ridden forward, but Cerdic grasped his rein.

Mago had not responded. His gaze was fixed upon the blue distance ahead. The Parthian stared into the impressive face of the explorer. He was uneasy. He had lost some of his bluster. "Have you no tongue in your head? Your silence betrays your guilt, bearded one. Then you must be a Roman spy!" He waited. There was no answer; not even a glance. He bit his lip. "Speak to me, Roman dog!" Silence. "You are our prisoners, do you understand? My father will make you talk." Silence. "There's a fine game he plays with Roman heads."

"We are neither Romans nor spies," Mago said eventually, "but simple merchants from Carthage, and we come as friends of the Parthian people."

"Friends!" The young Parthian, in one movement, un-ravelled his whip and sent it cutting across Mago's face. "How do you dare insult a Parthian by claiming his friendship?"

Suddenly Festus acted. "If Carthage will not avenge such an insult, then Rome will!" He dropped from his camel. Now he came running at the Parthian. He hurled a stone at the white stallion, causing it to twist and rear.

The Parthian held on skilfully. He drew a curved sword. His friends whooped. Their own weapons were out. There was to be sport after all. A second stone from Festus had caught the Parthian in the cheek, but Festus' cry pained him more:

"You'll be licking Roman shadows before this hour is through, Parthian cockerel!"

Furious, the youth lunged at Festus. His blade flashed at the Roman's head. Festus ducked. The other Parthians were swarming into the attack.

"Kill!" yelled their leader. "Spare none of them!"

Festus had seized the Parthian's purple cloak. "No Parthian is fit to wear a Roman cloak! From which corpse did you snatch it, thief?" Arms and bodies met in a flurry of blows. Holding off another swordcut, Festus dragged the Parthian from his horse. They fell together in a heap, rolling over twice. The Parthian's blade flickered towards Festus' side.

When three of the Parthian's friends rode in to assist him,

they collided with Cerdic, still mounted on his camel. The horses shrank back, repulsed less by the camel's weight and strength, than by its smell.

From the dust cloud that enveloped the combatants, Festus staggered up, panting for breath. But there was no movement from the Parthian. He lay on his stomach, his left arm outstretched. His right was bent under him, still holding the sword. A splash of blood touched the sand. Then a stream of it trickled from the sword-blade to handle. The gleaming white material was now soaked with blood.

Festus straightened in horror. "I didn't mean ... We struggled. I never touched his sword, never!"

All the action had stopped. There was silence again. The breeze began to build up a thin wall of sand against the Parthian's bleeding side. His friends retreated, boys once more, the taunting looks gone from their faces. The game was over.

Mago had dismounted. He turned the young victim on to his back. Blood spread over his hands. One glance was enough. He made no attempt to listen for the beating of the boy's heart. He raised his eyes for a long moment to Festus, but said nothing.

The Parthian clamour began again. The youths remembered their fathers' tents were not far off; that a Parthian had died at the hands of a Roman. They demanded Festus as a prisoner, and Festus, in dismay and sorrow at what he had done, was willing to go with them.

Mago ignored them. Though the Parthian was beyond medicine, his wound was bound up. He was placed across his white stallion. Mago's voice stilled the Parthian shouts.

"None of your fathers will believe that this boy brought on his own death, that it was a tragic accident. Destiny has come between us. Reason will no longer prevail, and only execution

awaits us if we delay." He slapped the Parthian's horse and
sent it galloping along the northern road. "Be gone, all of you!
And pray to the gods that we never meet again!"

Immediately the Parthians were out of sight, Mago ordered
the caravan to leave the road and cut due eastwards through
rough country. "If we have an hour's grace, we shall be
fortunate." Goading their beasts on with shouts and the crack
of the whip, they traversed a mountainous ridge of rocks which
led them into a valley whose sheer sides offered shade from the
scorching sun.

They ate in the saddle, stopping for only a few moments to
feed and water the animals. The landscape endlessly repeated
itself—crags honed to sharpness by wind and heat, hazardous
rock shelves, boulder-strewn sand and withered trees.

Wherever possible, the caravan crossed rock rather than
sand, so that tracks might be concealed. Mago ordered several
switches of direction, from east to south and then eastwards
again towards the mountains. Yet, to Cerdic's eyes the mountains never seemed to get any nearer.

The immense desert sun burst on ebony spearpoints of rock
and crimson light cascaded between the shadows.

Darkness brought no rest for the caravan. "We must ride
through the night," Mago insisted. "Take courage! Our efforts
will bring us all the sooner to the land beyond the North
Wind."

A numbing coolness followed the day's heat, and there
were many stumbles over unseen rocks. Thankfully the moon
rose into a clear sky, its golden sheen lighting the monotonous
way ahead.

Cerdic felt himself begin to shiver. The darkness was playing strange tricks with the landscape. It seemed to be moving, changing its shape, and he feared that at any second the ground would vanish from under him.

The thought entered his head that the Parthian boy's angry spirit rode beside them. Were those the dead one's whispers of accusation Cerdic could hear? He glanced at Festus, wrapped in shadow and his own sad thoughts. His friend had spoken only once: "It seems that the gods have cursed me, and misfortune flies before me wherever I go. I have brought disaster on Mago's caravan."

Cerdic had tried to find words that would give comfort to his friend. "You saved my uncle, Festus, remember that."

"Saved him? From a boy? No, I was rash and stupid . . . Mago should have delivered me up to the Parthians, then all would have been well."

Cerdic was dozing. The bumpy rhythm of the camel was rocking him to sleep. He fought to keep awake. "Think of something!" But only visions came, of the dying boy bleeding in the sand. "That purple cloak—perhaps he'd killed a Roman to get it."

Such thoughts did not make the Parthian's death any easier to bear. "Purple . . . *Purple.*" He latched on to the word. "Now Cerdic, my boy, pay attention! What has Mago told you about purple? Come on, sit up straight and don't talk as if you're chewing an olive . . ." He yawned. "The Romans, being of a very superstitious turn of mind, believe that purple keeps evil demons at bay and helps you win victories . . . as well as being very good for treating gnat bites . . . Purple!" His head was slumping forward again. "Is extracted from shellfish found along the shores of the Medit . . . Medit . . . whatever that sea is supposed to be called. Funny how it comes out yellow . . .

.. .

He was falling against the camel's neck. "And in the sunlight . . ." He was tumbling sideways. "It turns purp—."

Bump. He rolled in the sand and was still.

Bright morning. A wedge of goat's cheese and several grinning faces met Cerdic's first waking stare. Mago's hand was on his shoulder. "Was there ever a more useful blessing—to ride through the hours of darkness and still get a good night's sleep! Do you realise, Cerdic, you've been trussed like a haunch of beef to the back of a packhorse, and yet dreamt like a child in its cradle?"

"I was awake all the time," protested Cerdic. "It was just that I wanted to give the old camel a rest!"

They all laughed and felt their anxieties lighten a little.

The caravan had stopped behind a high, steep-sided outcrop of rocks, which offered a commanding view of the plain.

Festus, on look-out, called to Mago. "We are not the only travellers to pass this way. See the tracks? A caravan, about our size, I should imagine."

Mago welcomed this as good news. "In which direction, Festus?"

"North-west."

Thyrsis suddenly darted from his vantage point. "Parthians! They're coming!"

All eyes stared out. "So soon," said Mago. "They ride on wings of anger. How far off are they?"

"Five miles," guessed Thyrsis. He groaned. "There are scores of them. We are done for!"

"Not yet, my friend! Festus, take the animals. Thyrsis and Cerdic, go with him. Where our tracks cross into the rocks, lead the animals into the tracks of the other caravan. When you return, brush away their prints with branches."

33

Silence ruled the landscape. The wind had dropped. The only movements were of flies milling round the heads of the squatting camels, the nod of a head, the lazy flick of a tail.

Cerdic watched a bead of sweat form on Silenos' forehead. It trickled towards his sun-flushed nose. Thyrsis too was sweating. His palm shone as he laid his cold sword-blade in it. The fifteen carriers crouched close to the ground, motionless as the rocks.

"They're heading right for us," whispered Festus.

The Parthians approached through a shimmering heat haze. They seemed hardly to be moving along the baked earth; rather they appeared to be floating, drifting closer on a tide of light.

Mago gripped Hannibal's Leg. "One sound, my friends, and we are lost."

There were flashes of silver from the breastplates of the Parthians as they emerged from the haze. "You'd think they were hunting fully-armed Romans," murmured Thyrsis, "not a defenceless caravan."

Something on the rocks immediately below drew Cerdic's attention from the advancing horsemen. He nudged Festus. "Am I imagining things?" There, clearly exposed on a low rock not twenty feet from the track along which the horsemen would pass, was something metal, gleaming.

"It's a ladle! Silenos' cooking ladle!"

Festus beat the air with his fist. "They'll come straight for us." He was about to convey the news to Silenos of his tell-tale ladle, when Cerdic jammed a finger against his lips.

"Please don't tell him, Festus! What's the use? He's scared out of his wits already. It's a sure sign when he stuffs his mouth with olives—to stop his teeth chattering."

No more words. The Parthians were swooping down

34

between the far rocks, at least fifty of them, in light armour, carrying longbows and quivers of arrows slung across their backs. They were abreast of the caravan hidden high above them.

Cerdic pressed his knuckles between his teeth, too afraid even to breathe. They were passing. None looked up. None glanced at the gleaming ladle.

But where the caravan tracks merged and switched direction north-west, the Parthian leader halted his men. He too wore a purple cloak. He too rode a white stallion. He ordered his men to circle round, and several trotted back the way they had come, examining the animal tracks.

No jewel, thought Cerdic, could shine so brightly as that ladle. The horsemen had fanned out between the rocks. A few dismounted. Their voices found echoes. Even the chaffing of their arrows could be heard.

Festus' grip tightened on his sword. "Here comes one!" He was on the rock directly below that crowned by Silenos' ladle. He gazed across at the rocks opposite. Then he turned.

"He's seen it! No, wait." The man was climbing higher, staring directly at the wall which concealed the caravan. He backed a step to obtain a better view. He shared the rock with Silenos' ladle.

"He'll tread on it!"

The ladle was an arrow's length from his heel. He raised a hand to shield his eyes from the sun. He paused.

Cerdic's mouth was drier than the desert. He would not even permit his strained eyes to blink in case he missed a single movement of the Parthian.

A loud command came from the leader. He spurred his white stallion and waved for his men to follow.

On the rocks below the caravan, gleamed the ladle. On the

same rocks stood the Parthian. He still peered up, as though he could hear the heartbeat of his hidden enemy. He looked round. The ladle was at his very toes. He received a second command from his leader, and still he delayed.

Reluctantly, and with his eyes burning the rocks above, he obeyed orders. His shadow darkened the one clue that would have prevented the Parthians a wasted journey.

As swiftly as they had come, the Parthians were gone, heading north-west in a swirl of sand.

The members of the caravan were too gripped with shock to feel much relief. They knew full well that the Parthians would soon discover their mistake and return, resolved not to make another.

A comment from Silenos helped ease the tension—at least for Festus and Cerdic. Busying himself checking the loads, the fat cook had begun to scratch his head. "I'm wonderin'," he said, "whatever 'appened to me ladle . . ."

3

Hermit of the ruins

Convinced that the Parthians would not give up their pursuit, Mago persisted in leading the caravan a zig-zagging trail. One day the mountains seemed no more than an hour's ride away, then they faded again as the caravan tracked southwards.

Spirits were low. What talk there was concentrated on aches and pains, on sores caused by days of riding. Yet, since Festus the proud Roman refused to confess to the pains he suffered, Cerdic the stubborn Carthaginian was determined not to either. Exhausted, they pretended to each other that they were fresher at the end of the day than at the beginning.

When Silenos whined aloud, "Oh me posterior, me poor posterior's black and blue!" Festus forced himself to sing and Cerdic, though the pain from his raw blisters almost made him sick, strummed his harp.

"This is silly," he would say to himself. "We're doing it just to make the others admire us." But nothing in the world would make Cerdic admit it—not, that is, until Festus admitted it first; and Festus kept singing at the top of his voice.

Mago alone sustained their faith in the purpose of their journey. Tales of his travels shortened the hours and his vision of that undiscovered civilisation living beyond the mountains, beyond the deserts, beyond the North Wind, filled his listeners with wonder. "And remember, Carthage has put her faith in us. We cannot let her down."

The good cheer excited by Mago's decision finally to head due east, was abruptly dispelled when Festus rode up from his watching position behind the caravan. "More horsemen!"

For the present they were mere specks on the golden ridge of the horizon, but once again the caravan was cracked into a headlong pace. Sores were forgotten. Cerdic felt his heart beating as fast and as loudly as his camel's feet thumped over the sand.

Darkness had never been so welcome. It not only offered concealment but cooling winds from the mountains, and faint scents of distant pine forests.

The caravan had left the desert. It crossed a vast, ascending plateau of rock. About half a mile away, the rock appeared to spring up into a solid black wall. In the blackness, there were shapes. Festus reined his camel in surprise.

"What on earth . . . Cerdic, do you see it?"

They rode forward a little. "A city!" exclaimed Cerdic. "Towers, buildings . . ." He swung his camel round. "Uncle Mago, Uncle Mago!"

In amazement, the entire caravan had halted. As though magically risen from the black rock, what had seemed to Cerdic a city was revealed as a huge palace, its many towers spiking the sky.

"Not since the days of Alexander the Great, has there been a city in these parts," mused Mago, straining his weak eyes.

Cerdic and Festus had ridden on. They returned. "It's nothing but a ruin, Uncle. An empty shell."

"The towers you can see," explained Festus, "are giant pillars, of halls that are no more."

The caravan approached softly. Cerdic was afraid. The

ruined palace was a haunting sight. Its scores of pillars seemed to be lengthening into the sky, its broken walls about to fall into a thousand pieces.

Closer, and Cerdic could make out ramps, hundreds of yards long, joined by wide stone staircases. It was not sheer rock behind the palace, but the first of a line of foothills, the shape of massive furrows, leading to the mountains.

The darkness, as it had always done, made Cerdic tremble. He imagined warriors tall as the sky waiting in the shadows to leap upon him. There was not a space empty of menace and danger. He dismounted with the rest. He kept close to Festus. Mago was behind and yet he still sprang back in alarm at the images in front of him.

Festus pressed Cerdic's arm reassuringly. "They're only statues!" Carved in relief on the facing walls of the ramps and the staircases were soldiers on the march: bearded men with cruel mouths and eyes, in fluted hats and flowing costumes, carrying spears, bows and quivers. They were paying homage to a great king seated in majesty.

Mago had advanced alone. He traced the sculptures reverently with his hands. He turned, nodding his head. "This place, my friends, if I am not mistaken, is mighty Persepolis." He gazed about him, conjuring up in his mind the former grandeur of this dark ruin. "The palace flourished when the Assyrians were at the height of their power—conquerers of all Mesopotamia."

Momentarily, the pursuing Parthians were quite forgotten. "See!" Mago pointed towards the enthroned king. "Darius the Great, borne by his subject nations. And there is his son, Xerxes, who marched on Greece and was rebuffed by those gallant three hundred Spartan warriors at the Pass of Thermopilae ... A thousand years of history lies under our

39

feet!" He stood in rapt silence. "All gone, vanished—all their triumphs." He glanced slowly at Festus. "So will it be for Rome."

"Never!" responded Festus, yet half convinced that what Mago said was true.

"Alexander the Great returned here from his victories. Feasted here. Probably placed his foot on this very spot. They say that one night when he had drunk too much wine, he ordered the palace to be burnt to the ground."

"Aye," burst in Thyrsis impatiently, "and we'll be nothing but ashes if those Parthians catch up with us. This is no time for history lessons."

"You speak good sense, Thyrsis. We must hide in the ruins . . . We shall have need of stout Assyrian walls when the Parthians begin to fire their arrows."

Where kings and warriors and head-bowed captives had stepped became the route of camels and pack-horses; where carpets had once been laid for princely feet, fell camel droppings which it was Cerdic's task to clear so that the Parthians would find no trace of the caravan.

They passed into what Mago said must be the famous Hall of a Hundred Pillars. They trod through piles of cedar ash that had lain undisturbed for almost three hundred years.

At the heart of the ruined palace, they stopped. "Feed the animals, Thyrsis, and do you hear, Silenos—no fire tonight. We'll have to be content with a cold supper."

"Figs again!" sighed Festus. "If I die tonight I'm sure I'll grow into a six foot fig tree by morning."

"As a special treat," Silenos promised, "I'll be lettin' y' finish off that 'erdsman's beer, wi' 'ard boiled eggs an' green peppers."

Grateful for their first rest that day, the travellers sat with their backs to the stone walls, still warm from the sun's rays. Cerdic gazed at the jagged spikes of stone between the far pillars. There were figures of lions and bulls, and beautifully carved rosettes. "Will you be able to remember all this for your Log, Uncle Mago?"

"If we survive the night, my boy," replied Mago sadly. "In other circumstances, we would stay here a week, note down every detail before wind and decay rob the future of such riches." He brightened. "At least the Parthians have done one good thing—they have helped us to rediscover Persepolis!" Before going to consult Thyrsis about what possible defensive action the caravan should take, Mago told Cerdic that, when the kings were in residence, over fifteen thousand courtiers, soldiers, huntsmen, musicians and servants lived in the palace.

"Fancy having that number to feed, eh, Silenos?" said Cerdic.

But Silenos was not listening. Rather, he was shaking, from head to foot. He had been polishing his dishes and pots as he always did in idle moments. Then his fingers opened and a dish clattered on to stone. He did not stoop to retrieve it. He did not move, merely stared, mouth open, directly in front of him.

Then he gave voice to his terror. "May Jupiter protect us!" He sucked in his breath. He pointed. "A ghost!" All eyes followed his frozen stare.

On a far wall, starkly visible against the starlit sky, was a figure.

"A ghost!" repeated Silenos. "M-Master, help us!"

The figure was robed, and the robe swayed in the breeze from the mountains. "W-wearin' a crown . . . Carryin' a spear! Can't you see, Master?"

The ghost moved.

Silenos cast himself on to the ground with a hollow smack. "The gods save us!" he wailed.

As quickly as it had appeared, the figure vanished, to return moments later, bearing a lighted torch. It seemed to be walking the mountain edge. The high crown, ringed with jewels, and the sheen of the ghost's cloak, glowed in the wavering flame. A white, expressionless face floated forward on the shadows, haggard as a skull.

"It's coming towards us," bleated Silenos. "We must run!" Yet he was too frightened to stir a muscle. The carriers retreated.

"Wait!" commanded Mago, barring the carriers' way with Hannibal's Leg.

The ghost had raised its eerie white arms. There was a jangling sound as gold and silver ornaments dropped from its wrists.

"It's going to speak," whispered Festus, venturing a single step forward.

The voice came forth as from a cracked vessel, more like the night howl of a wolf than a human sound.

"Unfurl! Unfurl your Golden Banners! O countless host of the enemy, unfurl your shining gold! Be gone ye who drive us to death—be gone!" The figure leapt along the parapet, flames soaring after him. "Be gone, Golden Banners! Burn and die!"

Silenos' teeth were chattering almost as loud as his toes were knocking on the stone pavement; but Thyrsis was not so easily scared. He spoke calmly, "A madman, nothing more!" He drew his sword. "We must put out that torch before the Parthians ride down our throats."

"Wait, Thyrsis," said Mago. "I will speak with him. I have heard tell of these wonderful golden banners. The Parthians

42

fought with them at Carrhae. Shining banners, brighter than the sun, of a material never seen before in the West."

"Halt!" cried Silenos' ghost, Thyrsis' madman. "Who trespasses upon my kingdom? A thousand of your tribe will be executed for such disobedience."

Fear suddenly left Cerdic. Thyrsis was right. There stood a pathetic madman clad in wreaths of beads and bangles; and Cerdic was ready to laugh.

But Mago's voice was soft and respectful, meek as a courtier's. "We are poor strangers, Your Majesty, travelling from afar, and we bring you tribute."

Cerdic and Festus were grinning at one another.

"On to your knees, shepherds," commanded His Majesty, "for that is what I perceive you to be. If you are Parthian dogs, expect no mercy. I will have your heads on the spiked gates of my palace before dawn, and your Golden Banners will be dyed with Parthian blood."

"We are not Parthians, Your Majesty, but Citizens of Carthage and Rome."

"Rome, do you say?" His Majesty divested himself of a profound sigh. "Rome! Then you are right welcome to our palace. Persepolis greets you, humble guardians of the gentle sheep. Break bread at my table, eat of the succulent hind, drink the sweet mead of the southern isles—all my bounty is yours. Set the tables, slaves!" He waved his torch to urge on his invisible servants. "Summon the jugglers and clowns. We shall have conjuring, and for every golden banner drawn from the hat, I will show you the secrets of the enemy strength."

Even Silenos had lost his fear. He was chuckling, his fat chins shaking in merriment and relief. "I'm wonderin' if 'is Majesty's got some dancin' girls 'idden up 'is sleeve."

"It is auspicious, shepherds," continued his Majesty, "That

you have found me still in the palace, for by the first flush of dawn I and my legions will march east, over the mountains, to the land where the magical banners are woven. I, Widuhar, the lowly-born, but under a star of destiny. I who spiked the Parthian horse, and was left bleeding and near to death on the field of Carrhae—yes, I rose to be emperor on the throne of mighty Cyrus and Darius. Assyria lives! The great empire of the Persians will be reborn—once I discover the secret of the Golden Banners."

His speech at an end, he lowered his arms. He held out his torch, rather wearily, to scrutinise his visitors. Then, in a small, unkingly voice, he said, "I'm famished. You've not a bite or two to spare, by any chance?"

"If you douse that torch, Your Majesty," replied Mago, "we can provide you with simple shepherd's fare. But we fear the Parthians are on our heels, bringing with them the golden banners."

"No, impossible! I have destroyed them, every one! I, Widuhar the Immortal. A morsel of cheese, have you, and a cup of wine?"

At Mago's nod, Widuhar lowered his torch and cast it into the cedar ash on the hall floor. "Then you are granted our royal protection. The Prince of Persepolis bids you rise from your knees if you have not already done so."

His Majesty squatted unceremoniously among his new friends, and equally unceremoniously began stuffing dates, olives, goat's cheese and oatbread into his mouth with both hands, at the same time endeavouring to take huge swigs from a wine cup. "Ah," he said, with a strident belch, "this makes a refreshing change from all the suckling pig, stewed lamb, roast duckling, oysters, truffles, white fish, pears, peaches and pomegranates which my fifty cooks serve me every day."

It transpired that King Widuhar had ruled at Persepolis for over ten years. He had sought refuge there from the Golden Banners. "They were everywhere!" His mind was haunted by that terrible battle so long ago. "They blocked the sun from our gaze. We fought in darkness, and that's how Surena and his Parthians managed to defeat us. Elephants, he had, to carry their supplies of deadly arrows."

After a brief, brooding silence, Widuhar said confidentially, "I received a message the other day from Jupiter himself . . . or was it Mars? I can't quite recall. But do you know what it said? That our general, Marcus Crassus, still waits to cross the Styx. Old Charon refuses him passage. Was there ever such a fool led Romans into battle?"

"Your Majesty," asked Festus, nervous but eager, "if you fought at Carrhae, did you ever know one Marinius, a Centurion?"

"Whether I knew him or not," replied Widuhar, "makes no odds now. All who fought at Carrhae are dead, save I alone . . ."

He paused and suddenly lowered his voice, glancing suspiciously from side to side. "Except, that is, for the—" He broke off. "Promise you will tell no one!"

"We promise," Mago assured him.

"Then for your welcome food and wine, I shall tell you. My own countless legions are nothing in comparison with the . . . you'll not tell?"

"We swear it."

His voice was hushed. "The Host of a Thousand, chosen by Mars himself from the dying sons of Rome. In the midst of the battle, the war-god swooped like an eagle into the Parthian ranks. Each of the thousand warriors he touched with his rod

45

of immortal strength sprouted wings and soared from that blood-drenched scene."

Thyrsis burst in. "Why are we delaying here, listening to this madman's fantasies when the Parthians are almost upon us?"

"It is true what I say! And when the Host stream from their mountain palace in the East, all Parthia trembles." Widuhar sprang up. "As your pursuers will do now." He was all at once master of his wits. "I will help you—if you will take me from this place. It is so lonely being emperor of millions." The Lord of Persepolis looked very much as though he was going to burst into tears. "So very, very lonely . . . Come! Tread silently and bring your flocks of sheep."

"Sheep?" echoed Silenos.

"Obey his actions," advised Mago, "not his words. He is our only chance."

Widuhar led them from the ruined hall along stone passages whose roofs were the stars. Cerdic gripped his uncle's arm. Nothing but a swordcut would have made him let go. The breeze dislodged a scattering of plaster from a broken stone column. "Courage, my boy," soothed Mago as Cerdic started.

Circling a stepped pyramid of stone, they descended a ramp towards the mouth of an underground doorway, partly blocked by fallen masonry. Festus and Tryphon helped Widuhar to swing open the double stone doors. "Inside!" ordered Widuhar. "Here is where I usually keep my harem of pretty wenches, whom this very day I despatched in two hundred wagons with my armies to the East."

As the doors were being closed behind them, Thyrsis protested. "How can we trust him? We're trapped. He could sell our heads to the Parthians."

Widuhar halted, the great iron rings of the doors clinking in his hands. "Betray Romans?" he said, aghast. "And bring upon

46

myself the wrath of the Host?" He laughed. "Do you take the Prince of Persepolis for a madman?" He hurled the doors to.

The minutes of waiting were like hours. Not a word was spoken. The darkness kept everyone standing exactly where he had been when the doors were shut. The only sound, scarcely audible, was that of ash and stone chippings blown across the courtyard above.

When Cerdic's eyes finally adjusted to the darkness, he noticed a slit window high up on the far wall. "Festus," he whispered. "Give me a leg up to that window." Grateful for something to do, Festus inched to the wall, his arms outstretched. He leaned against rough stone, his hands cupped. Cerdic was up and on his shoulders. "Can you see anything?"

What caught Cerdic's attention the instant he looked out of the slit window he was reluctant to describe, for it would have filled his companions with dismay.

There, in the most prominent spot he could have chosen, stood Widuhar, Prince of Persepolis, with his torch re-lighted, and waving it high above his head so that the whole Parthian nation would see it.

"What's happening, then?" Festus inquired impatiently.

"Very little really." Cerdic felt terrible.

"You're shaking, what's the matter? Come on, let me have a look."

"You're too heavy for me to hold, and anyway, I've special sort of eyes that can see in the dark."

"There seems to be a light coming in from somewhere."

"You must be imagining things. A meteor, perhaps, dashing through the heavens." Cerdic glanced out again. He swallowed hard, for over the distant brow of stone, the Parthians appeared. They were on foot, their swords drawn, as startled as

47

Mago and his followers had been at the sight of Widuhar, who was aglitter with jewels and holding a dancing beacon of fire in that palace of the dead.

Now everyone became aware that Widuhar was no longer in hiding. He began to shout. "Tell us!" demanded Festus, giving Cerdic's leg a fierce nip. "Or let me see for myself."

"Ssh! He's addressing the Parthians. They're not sure what to make of him."

Some of the Parthians had edged away, but their leader held his ground. He spoke to Widuhar and was answered by a sweep of the madman's arm. Cerdic caught his breath; was Widuhar pointing to the caravan's hiding place?

"Come down," barked Thyrsis, "if you can say nothing." His nerve was snapping. "We're like caged beasts, bought and sold . . . I for one shall not die like this," He strode towards the door. "If we are to fight, then let us not delay."

"You will be the death of us all, Thyrsis," growled Mago, his formidable shape barring Thyrsis' way. "One more step and my staff awaits you!"

Thyrsis relented. He swung through the dark and cast himself into a corner, biting his nails.

When Cerdic glanced out again, he could see nothing, not even the glow of Widuhar's torch. He waited. There was no sound. The madman could have agreed to lead them to his prisoners. Only when the doors opened would the fate of the caravan be known.

"Lower me down, Festus. They've left the ramp together, and I think they're coming in our direction."

Unknown hands were laid on the iron rings of the doors. The rings rattled and squealed as they turned. Cerdic crossed to Mago whose arm closed protectively around him. Festus and Thyrsis stood with their swords drawn, Tryphon beside them, armed with a javelin. Even Silenos had found courage enough to raise his cooking ladle.

The doors swung open. There was a yell, a movement—and in marched the Prince of Persepolis. Alone.

"You may step forth in safety, shepherds," declared Widuhar. "Your enemies have fled like dogs with their tails between their legs. Villains all! I spit on them!"

"Fled?" answered Mago warily. "But how did you persuade them?"

"By informing them of the recent whereabouts of Mars' glorious warriors—the Host of a Thousand . . . In these parts, O doubtful ones, the Host is no laughing matter. They descend like lightning with their hearts full of vengeance, and not even the Golden Banners can halt their destruction. What can poor Parthians do but flee at the very sound of their name?"

Widuhar gave a cough, and there was a sly look in his eyes. "I also informed the rogues that a caravan led by a black-bearded merchant had passed north not five hours before!"

"Then the road to the mountains, and the East, lies open to us," said Mago joyfully.

"Thanks be to the Host!" roared the Prince of Persepolis.

4

Mountains that vanish into the sky

Each time Cerdic wiped the sweat from his eyes, more trickled from his hair, almost blinding him. He was grateful for a brief rest—but what a place to be resting in! Taking a deep gulp of mountain air, and leaning his back hard against the rock, he dared himself to glance down.

"Please let this be a dream!" Above him and below was a sheer wall of rock. Mago's caravan was straddled on a ledge scarcely wide enough for two men to pass. The one route across the mountain range, this ledge ascended into dense mist. Parts of the surface had been built out over the void by the mountain people, using wooden wedges and broken stones.

"Keep your eyes looking upwards," Mago had instructed, and Cerdic had followed his uncle's advice. Until now. His boot dislodged a pebble. It spun into empty space—down, down—touching nothing that could have offered succour to a falling man. The drop was incalculable. Twenty tall towers, thought Cerdic, stood one upon the other, would not reach him from the thundering torrent of water below, itself imprisoned between vertical banks.

Cerdic eased himself on to his haunches. He looked outwards—mist and more precipitous mountain faces. Uncle

Mago's failing eyesight had been a serious handicap on the way up. He miscalculated distances and failed to discern slippery from dry stone. Several times, Cerdic in front and Tryphon behind, had needed to steady Mago when he lost balance. Once he had stumbled full on his face.

Before the day's climb had begun, Thyrsis had quarrelled with Mago. He was not afraid of the mountains, nor of narrow tracks that seemed to vanish into the sky—but what was the point? In the foothill village where Mago had hired a young guide called Haji, and haggled over the exchange of his camels for mountain mules, or yaks, Thyrsis had listened to stories. Beyond the mountains, he was told (through His Majesty King Widuhar, who understood the people's language) there was nothing but a whirlwind of poisonous gases concealing a pit cut through the very centre of the earth.

Mago had replied shrewdly. "And have you not asked the mountain folk what lies west of the Parthian desert, Thyrsis? They might tell you of a monstrous serpent coiled five times round the Mediterranean Sea, giving forth a stench more nauseous than the sewers of Rome."

There was laughter but Thyrsis did not give up. "Then what of the bandits? Can we risk them being mere inventions to frighten off innocent travellers? They sound real enough, lying in wait to throw boulders from the cliffs. They rob and then they cut the throats of their victims. We should have hired armed men, Mago, for how can we defend ourselves?"

Mago had stroked his black beard. He had smiled and waved a long bony hand in the direction they had come. "What alternative have we, Thyrsis my friend? If you are a galley slave, you either bear the whip or take to the open sea and drown. Return, and the Parthians will surely slit our throats.

51

Go forward, and who knows what treasures may lie beyond the Onion Mountains?"

"Your kind of treasures, maybe," grumbled Thyrsis. "But not my kind—not gold."

"Gold?" came in Widuhar. "There'll be plenty of gold once we find the sources of the banners that flame in the morning sun. The Host have them. Yes! We shall tap three times on the great onion slopes, and three times more. Out will ride the Host of a Thousand!"

Cerdic's sweat had dried. The mountain wind drove icily against his tunic. He huddled into himself and was glad when Mago ordered the caravan to move forward again. The air grew thinner as they climbed, more difficult to breathe, and through the wind Cerdic could hear the others puffing and gasping.

Occasionally rocks slipped from the mist above and tumbled, in clouds of grit, into the angry waters below. The wind discovered Cerdic's harp, playing a strange melody.

To divert his thoughts from the giddy emptiness beneath, Cerdic dwelt on the journey so far. There had been the mountains east of Persepolis. They had seemed so high and dangerous, yet, thought Cerdic, they were molehills compared to the giant mountains they were climbing now.

Then there had been a thirty-day passage across dust-dry plains. And what a trip that was! Horrible sores, smarting eyes, and water tasting like cat's pee ... Yet Uncle Mago always found something interesting to write in his Log.

The great Onion Mountains, as the local people called them, because of the scent of onions that came off the foothills, had been quick to offer Cerdic a greeting—in the form of a wild goat which had chased, and caught him, leaving two unsightly scars on his rear.

"Still, there've been plenty of good things, despite that goat.

To lie flat on your back after a hard day's march and just stare up at the sky. Have a bath in a mountain stream. Smell the charcoal from old Silenos' fire. Watch the sunlight fade over the hills. It's better than school or learning to be a soldier."

He was remembering valleys of orchards, sweet pears, meadows bright with yellow mustard; and he was remembering the comforting firelight round which the travellers gathered each evening, to swap tales, to sing or to hear a tune on the harp. Then there was the moment when they retired to their pyramid-shaped skin tents, to nestle into warm sleeping bags and listen to the howl of the night wind.

Cerdic could not prevent his thoughts returning to the steepening track ahead. So long as it was a ledge hewn from the rock itself, he felt reasonably safe. He trembled, though, when he saw the track extend from the face, with nothing but empty air below it.

The incident he had imagined now happened. The tragedy was sudden. From beginning to end, it took no more than three or four seconds.

About half the yaks had passed a section of built-up track, when, all at once, the road disintegrated. Stones shot away from beneath the feet of a mule that had been with the caravan from its first day on Syrian soil. Admiral Pompey, Cerdic had named it. Now Pompey fell, dragging one of the hired carriers with it.

Both fought desperately to tread the moving stones. But they were in space, falling. There was a cry from the man, a dim, startled cry, as though he could not believe that death could strike so quickly. Then they were no longer man and beast but dark objects spinning through air; and the torrent below received them with no more ceremony than it would a lifeless rock.

The caravan was divided by a gap in the track some three paces wide, with Mago, Cerdic, Tryphon and the guide, Haji, above, and the rest below. "We must build the path up as it was," shouted Mago through the wind and the mist.

Haji was shaking his head. "What is he saying, Widuhar?"

King Widuhar translated. "Haji says that the path's got to be built up by the mountain folk, and blessed by their priest, or the gods will be displeased."

"Tell Haji—I have gifts for his gods that will soothe their anger."

Thyrsis was calling from below. "We must return for help, Mago. It's no use going on."

"Return for help? no! It would take you hours to get back to the village. Nightfall is not far off and we would freeze to death by morning."

"It's the only way," shouted Thyrsis. "I said all along we were inviting disaster."

Last in line, Festus acted decisively. He drew his sword. "No one returns! Do you understand, Thyrsis? You will have to kill me to pass."

Mago was giving Cerdic instructions. "Take the javelins from the second yak, my boy—carefully now!" Even this simple action was perilous on the mountain face, for Cerdic had to pass one of the carriers who had crouched down in fear and refused to make room. Cerdic was forced to step over him. He saw the gaping space behind him. It seemed to be calling to him: you will fall, fall, slip and fall.

"Steady the beast first, Cerdic. Gently, stroke his head. In my Bag of Tricks, reach for the coil of fine rope. You have it? Good. Next, the iron mallet and my Cyclops nails—you remember, the ones with the eye in them."

Festus appeared on the other edge of the divide. "Let me

help, Mago." His apparent calm concealed a turmoil of feelings. On what he did in the next few minutes, lives would depend, and he had little faith in himself.

"Give way, this is man's work," cried Thyrsis, coming forward. He was stung at the thought that his companions might believe he had intended to desert them.

Nothing could have persuaded Festus to change his mind. "Do you take me for a coward? I am a Roman!"

Mago explained that in order to build the path up again, javelins would have to be driven into the rock below the level of the path. "Which of you two volunteers is willing to swing on a rope?"

Cerdic and Festus eyed each other nervously. "I'll do it," resolved Festus. "I'm older." And Cerdic, who had no head for heights, felt a great sense of relief. This was one of the times when not being a man was an advantage.

But there were tasks to perform. As Festus was tying the rope-end around his waist, Cerdic handed his uncle the mallet, then a few of the Cyclops nails. He watched Mago lean out across the divide. His throat was dry. His heart thumped.

Slowly Mago drove the nail deep into the rock until only the Cyclops' eye was visible. Festus leaned out too and, waveringly, and at the third attempt, threaded the end of the rope through the Cyclops' eye.

"Will just one nail hold Festus' weight, Uncle?"

"Such a nail has taken my burden often enough. Don't you remember how I swung from that cliff-edge in Northern Africa, gathering gannets' eggs? If the knot is secure, Festus, lower yourself slowly below the path. We'll keep the rope taut. Try to find a foothold, but we have you safe if you slip."

Festus obeyed. Could they hear his teeth betraying him as a coward? He prayed to the spirit of his dead elder brother:

55

"Help me, Gaius! Help me not to make a mess of it. Or if I do, let me die." He squatted down. He turned, reaching outwards blindly for a foothold. He had still to let go. His hands refused to release their grip on the path.

"Just below you, Festus," suggested Cerdic, "a ledge. No, a little to the left."

Festus tested the ledge. He was half way there. Had the roar of the waters got louder? An inner voice taunted him: "You're not going to be able to do it." In answer, and with great determination, he kicked out towards the ledge, no wider than a sword-blade, but the only possible foothold.

His entire body was over the edge. He slipped down. His toe stubbed against the ledge. He gasped. There were frightened cries from above. He was swinging helplessly over the void. "I can't!" he yelled in terror.

"Pull him up," rapped Thyrsis.

"I'm proud of you, Festus," said Mago, his deep voice giving confidence. "That took real courage. Don't look down. Don't think of the drop. Concentrate on finding yourself a foothold."

"Again to your left," came in Cerdic.

Festus grunted. He sensed a sudden thrill of pride. Hand and foot found somewhere to lodge. He eased his weight off the rope. "Now what?"

Cerdic had dropped on to his chest. He held out his uncle's iron mallet.

"Got it, Festus?"

"Right."

Mago continued his instructions. "Cerdic will hand you the javelins. They've a good sharp point and you must hammer them into the rock at this angle—can you see?" Mago outlined a 45 degree angle with his arms.

The javelins were wooden hafted, shorter than those used by the Romans in battle, designed and made by Mago himself.

Festus was confident, almost cheerful. He took a moment to decide which was the best grip on the heavy mallet. He reached for the first javelin almost carelessly—and paid the penalty. The javelin slipped from his fingers and fell through the mist.

"Oh Mago, I'm sorry!" Another inner voice attacked him cruelly: "You're a fool! You can't be trusted with anything. What father could possibly be proud of you?"

"Steady," soothed Mago.

The second javelin Festus held firm. He placed its point down against the rock. He was angry with himself and his anger reinforced his hammer blows. Indeed he struck at the butt of the javelin so hard that he hurled himself from his ledge and crashed into the mountain wall.

There were voices from above, but he did not hear them. It was as though he was in battle. He attacked the javelin and it sunk home. He snatched another. These were Parthians he was knocking into the next life; those who had imprisoned his father, those who had cut out good Tryphon's tongue. Soon, eight javelins quivered in line.

"Splendid, Festus!" called Mago. "Your father Marinius would be proud of you this day . . . Ready for the next stage?"

Festus nodded, smiling but fierce; in the terrible cold, he was warm as an oven. Eight more javelins were struck into the rock, this time on a line with the track edge. Their hafts met the other javelins which, when Festus bound them together with cord, formed a firm bracket against the mountain.

While Festus had been busy driving in the final javelins, Thyrsis and Widuhar had unhooked the caravan's tents from the yaks. "Remove the centre-poles," shouted Mago across the divide, "and lay them over the javelins . . . Be sure, Festus, to tie them securely. Next, our firewood!"

Despite his huge bulk, half of which extended over the precipice, Silenos was determined to help. Gasping for breath, he unloaded the considerable store of firewood and handed it up, piece by piece, to Tryphon. "Mind you drops none, Festus. It's worth more'n gold to us."

Having bound the centre-poles to the brackets of javelins, Festus lashed the sturdy pieces of fresh-cut wood across the centre-poles. He felt like singing. He had done it. He, Festus, not Gaius. He tugged on the rope and was hauled up. No one had ever cheered him before, but the whole caravan did so now—including Thyrsis. "Not bad for a young 'un," he admitted.

"Stand with your backs to the rock everyone," ordered Mago. "The designer of such a risky bridge must be the first to prove its strength."

But Cerdic was grasping Mago's hand and would not let it go. "Together, Uncle!" They inched forward. One strip of firewood snapped. The others held. The centre-poles groaned a little but the javelins stayed firm. Another cheer went up— they were across.

"Advance!" roared Mago. "And tonight Silenos will prepare us a feast in celebration."

With some nervous hesitations, more on the part of the carriers than the sure-footed yaks, the caravan passed to safety. But their journey was not to continue immediately. "At the risk of displeasing the mountain gods," Mago declared, "Our bridge must be dismantled . . . By the look of the storm clouds ahead, we shall be needing our tentpoles and firewood more than the gods will need this bridge."

The mountain track continued to rise and rise, until the

ledges jutting from the rock face were white with snow. Breath became clouds of steam. No amount of exercise created more than a dampening of sweat. The icy wind penetrated to the bone.

But Mago cheered the travellers on. He sang one of his own songs, about a land where there was a fountain of green jade, said to possess the gift of everlasting life:

Monarchs and beggars alike, what haste they made
To the merry Fountain of Jade!
But alas to tell, neither poet nor clown,
Lived long enough to pass the secret down!

Almost unnoticed, the cliff journey came to an end. The track dipped, the sheer slopes broke back on themselves, transformed first into easy gradients enveloped by mist, then patched with islands of grass. The sound of the torrent faded beyond rock-encrusted hills covered with mauve and purple heather.

At the bottom of a beautiful green valley stretched a rain-water lake. How good it felt, thought Cerdic, to be able to run free, released from the risk of falling stones; how good not to have to hang on to rocks full of sharp points, to dash through the first spring grass, to smell the scent of flowers growing at the lake's edge.

Festus was calling after him. "Swim!" They ran, the wind in their ears and their hair. Hot and sticky, they plunged into the crystal coolness of the water. They ducked and splashed. They glided down green glades shot through with the last gleams of afternoon sun.

Cerdic fished a smooth grey rock from the water and held it

up, glistening. "For Uncle's museum. It's a seashell buried in the stone—a fossil."

Festus laughed. "A seashell up in the mountains?"

"True—look! Uncle says that millions of years ago mountains such as these lay under the sea. Then great forces in the earth pushed them upwards."

Festus shook the water from his hair and the drops fell like jewels on the golden surface of the lake. "Mago's a wonderful man."

Cerdic nodded. He spoke sadly. "Soon he'll be a blind man—his eyes grow weaker every day."

"That won't make him turn back, though, will it?"

"When he's found the People Beyond the North Wind, then he'll return. Mago's name will go down in the history books . . . Just think, generations of schoolkids will have to write pages and pages about his discoveries! He'll be as famous as Carthage's greatest explorer, Hanno."

The brisk wind—and another race up the far shore of the lake—soon dried the two friends. It was time to return and help the others erect the tents, and they were circling round to the caravan when Cerdic stopped. He stared up at the bare ridge directly above them—bare, that is, save for a curious shape in silhouette against the dying sun.

They went nearer. It was a cairn of stones, built by the hand of man. There was another shape sticking out of the top of the cairn, difficult to identify from the angle Cerdic and Festus approached.

A few more paces and—

"A sword hilt!" cried Festus. He broke into a run. "It's a grave!"

The sword in the cairn cast a crooked shadow over the uneven ground. "Well this didn't arrive here millions of years ago, Cerdic . . . That's a Roman sword, I'm certain of it!"

The cairn was covered in moss and the sword was completely rusted. "It must have been here ages, though," mused Cerdic. "Here's something else!" He dropped to his knees and began to scratch at a flat stone embedded in the centre of the cairn.

They yelled together in excitement as a roughly inscribed letter appeared under the moss. They attacked the stone with their fingernails.

"Words—in Latin!" Festus' voice was hushed. "But how . . . how could this be possible? A Roman grave in these mountains? Other explorers, do you think?"

A name had emerged from the mossy stone: GAIUS.

"NOBLY FIGHTING," spelled out Cerdic, revealing the lower part of the epitaph.

"GAIUS CATO," continued Festus.

Slowly, and in amazement, the two friends uncovered the entire inscription. Together, they read it out:

GAIUS CATO

OF THOSE WHO SURVIVED THE PARTHIANS AT CARRHAE

DIED HERE, NOBLY FIGHTING.

For many moments, they sat in silence. The light had almost gone. The epitaph could only be read by the touch of fingers. Festus whispered the words into the advancing darkness, "Of those who survived the Parthians at Carrhae. Could this Gaius have fought side by side with my father?" He shook his head bitterly. "Yet there's no date on the inscription."

Cerdic felt he understood: after all, in these vast mountains, what significance had time? "Perhaps whoever cut the inscription didn't even know what year it was."

"What are we to make of this, Cerdic? Have I cause to hope?"

"I'm wondering," Cerdic replied, reverently touching the rusted sword, "whether here lies one of the Host of a Thousand."

Festus' eyes shone. "Could it be that there's some truth in Widuhar's ravings?" He stood up, resolute. "One thing's for sure: the gods have given us a sign. I feel it in my heart and in my bones—my father lives!"

5

Bandits

To begin with, it had whispered urgently across the lake, furrowing the reeds and sedge grass; then it blustered, humming louder and louder—a wind that set the tents of the caravan billowing like the sails of a ship in a storm. In spite of the heavy stones placed round the walls of the tents, skins were torn free and flapped noisily in the dark.

Cerdic awoke from the warm sheepskin sleeping bag his uncle had made for him. The hail came, so heavily upon the tent that the spatter of ice-pellets merged into a continuous roar. How swift was the anger of the mountains, he thought. The evening had been peaceful. There had been a touch of warmth in the air which heralded spring. Everyone felt it and the caravan had celebrated as though their journey was over, not just beginning.

Silenos had feasted them royally: roast suckling pig served in a tasty sauce seasoned with peppers and shallots followed by pancakes dipped in honey. "Eat well, my friends," Mago had said, "for our fare in future will be more that of prisoners than kings." They drank the sweet, syrupy wine of Marsala, and they sang around the cheerful fire.

By torchlight, they had all examined the grave of Gaius the Roman.

"Did I not tell you?" Widuhar had cried. "We tread the

path of the Host." His words seemed to scare him. "But they must not know of our coming . . . If they should suspect that I, Widuhar the Glorious, have left the portals of Persepolis in search of the Golden Banners—we would all be doomed." He paused. "Doomed! They would ride out of their gates in the mighty Onion Mountain and . . . and gallop to the moon. Yes, do not doubt me, shepherds, but I have it on good evidence that the Host can ride to the moon and back in the blinking of an eye . . . What a tragedy for us if they planted the Golden Banners there!" He had raised his finger to his lips. "The Lord of Persepolis advises silence. Not a word of the Host, for even our whispers might reach them."

But Widuhar's rule of silence did not satisfy Festus. He wanted to know what Mago thought, and Mago had given him a slender hope.

"Unless the Romans truly did gallop to the moon, it is clear they did not return West—at least not along the route we came. Haji, our guide, does not remember Romans, and none of the villagers spoke of them. That is all we can guess for the moment."

Thoughts too, dwelt upon the Land Beyond the North Wind and, as the sweet wine flowed, Mago had said, "My knowledge is like a huge map carved in stone, a map shattered into fragments. Over a lifetime of travels, I have picked up the pieces. Some fit together, some are real, some imaginary . . . It is a country whose size one can scarcely comprehend, of plains ringed by mountains and crossed by meandering rivers of yellow water. I see forests of ships, cities with gleaming roofs resounding to the ring of thousands of bells, and I see a wall, a great wall passing like a girdle about this country, built over the plains, across the deserts and even over the mountain ranges . . . I see machines, inventions, which we in the West have not yet dreamed of; and always I see books and I hear music."

"And the Banners," broke in Widuhar, "do you see the Banners?"

"Perhaps not the banners," Mago had replied. "But the cloth from which the banners were made—yes, that is a possibility."

Cerdic began to doze. The storm increased in fury, its aim to uproot the tents and hurl them into the distant gorge. One of Mago's stories lingered in his head, of how the People Beyond the North Wind believed their universe had begun. Assisted by a dragon, a unicorn, a phoenix and a tortoise, the great Creator had laboured for eighteen thousand years chiselling the earth into its present shape; and when the Creator died, so the story went, a wonderful transformation took place: his body became the soil of the world, his blood its rivers, his sweat the rain, his hair the trees and plants. His left eye turned into the sun, his right eye into the moon. His breath became the wind, his voice the thunder—and the parasites feeding on his body became the human race!

"Well," thought Cerdic in his half-sleep, "the breath of the Creator is blowing angrily now."

For several days the caravan followed the course of the river, still captive in its steep-walled ravine. The track wound ever upwards. The crest of one hill was a mere prologue to a higher one, and always there were more crests to climb and more mountains beyond, each a giant until it was belittled by another.

As it must have been for the Romans who inscribed no date on Gaius' grave, time came to have no meaning for the travellers. The days were the same: de-camping by dawn, slow, serpentine progress, a break when the sun touched the middle of the sky, erecting of tents before twilight, food, tales around the fire and early to sleep.

Yet for Mago the days seemed to provide infinite variety, and Cerdic soon grew to look eagerly forward to reading his uncle's fascinating Log of the journey.

In his tiny script, with his eyes close to the parchment, Mago described the terrain in every detail. He noted the crystals in the rock and the fossil remains, hazarding guesses as to their age. He gathered specimens of flowers and plants; he did sketches of them, and he was keen to hear from Cerdic and Festus of the birds and animals they saw.

As well as Mago's observations, there were his thoughts about the discoveries that might lie ahead of them. Though in his conversation he spoke of the People Beyond the North Wind, in his Log he referred to them as the "Seres". They were a very industrious people, he said, lovers of home and family. He referred to a poem once told him by a traveller, thought to be written by a Seric soldier, about how he longed to leave his lonely outpost and return for ever to his warm hearth.

Mago also wrote a footnote on Widuhar's Golden Banners: "This 'gold' of which Widuhar speaks, is real enough. At Carrhae the Parthian banners were made of a cloth very probably manufactured by the Seres. This Sericum, as we might call it, is smooth to the touch and possesses a miraculous sheen. How the cloth is made, is a secret, but it is a fact that merchants traversing the Indian Ocean are willing to take great risks to obtain it."

The caravan had encountered few human settlements, and none of them permanent: "The mountain people have welcomed us generously, offering us the best of their meagre rations. In exchange we have given them ornaments, strong rope, and a little invention of mine—wooden clasps, which the women of the tribes have greatly praised. The clasps prevent their laundered clothes scattering from the line in the mountain wind."

Most interesting were the stories the villagers told of warriors from the region of the setting sun: "There can be no question that Romans have passed this way. The people describe their armour and their shields, but their estimates of the Roman numbers vary from five thousand to not more than a hundred. They stayed only briefly—but long enough to repay the villagers' hospitality by routing a nest of mountain bandits who had terrorised the neighbourhood for years. Two years, five years, ten years? How long since, the villagers cannot remember. Their story matches Widuhar's, that the warriors vanished into the side of the great Onion Mountain.

"Of the Seres," recorded Mago, "the mountain people know nothing. Rather they speak of another people to the East and the North, whom they call the Faceless Ones, a race of horsemen who kill and burn, who put down no roots. The villagers speak of the Fire King who leads the Faceless Ones. His very name fills them with terror. They say that, to prove himself the chosen one of the gods, he built a fire that could be seen from one end of the great desert to the other. Then he stepped into the flames and was not harmed. When the fire died around him, the king remained alight, the flames issuing from his body—as they have done ever since."

"Uncle Mago," Cerdic said, when he had finished reading his uncle's Log, "do you really believe such tales—of a king who could stand in the flames and not be burnt?"

Mago had taken a few moments to consider his answer. "Within the bright shell of fancy there's often a kernel of truth.

No tale is so fantastic that an explorer should discredit it. Otherwise, would my fellow Carthaginian, Hanno, have persisted in his searches in Africa for the freakish tribe of men three feet tall? Yet he brought back ample proof of their existence.

"Or take as an example, Nearchos, valiant captain of Alexander, and one of the greatest explorers. There was an island he wished to visit, called Nosala, sacred to the sun. But the local people said that any man who set foot there vanished and was never seen again. Despite the terror of his sailors, Nearchos put ashore—and found many fine turtles which the natives were anxious to protect for their own consumption. Instead of vanishing, Nearchos and his men feasted on turtle!"

The sensation that the caravan was being watched by hidden eyes had grown all day. The travellers had been warned of bandits by the villagers and the fears of Haji, the guide, began to be shared by everyone.

Nerves were on edge. Thyrsis declared that he did not trust Haji. "How do we know he is not leading us straight on to the bandits' swords?"

"I trust the boy," replied Mago confidently. "For our sake, he risked the displeasure of his mountain gods."

"But he's misled us. According to him we were to cross the gorge within twenty days' marching. We have gone thirty days, yet where is this rope bridge he spoke of?"

"Be patient, Thyrsis."

"I'm in no mood for patience. For days we have struggled in and out of snowdrifts. We travel so slowly that yesterday's camp can be seen from today's."

"That is because the winter refuses to abandon the land."

Thyrsis was not listening. "And this mountain pass that will lead us into warm plains rich with crops and fruit—what is that but a dream?"

Mago's reply was cut off by Silenos who emitted a sudden yelp of fear. "Bandits! I seen one!" He was trembling. "Across t' gorge, more like an ape than a 'uman. T' gods give us succour!"

When all eyes followed Silenos' pointing arm, there was nothing. "I seen 'im, I swear it!"

"The bandits are there all right," agreed Thyrsis. "Behind every rock and tree."

Festus flung round on him. "Be silent, Thyrsis! Would you fill every heart with panic?"

Thyrsis went for his sword. Before he could draw it from the scabbard, he felt Mago's staff descend on his forearm. "Festus speaks sound sense, my friend. If your hand aches to strike a blow in anger, wait—for the bandits will no doubt put it to the test soon enough."

Unaware of the doubts that had been cast upon his faithfulness, Haji had waved for the caravan to stop. He shouted gleefully. "What is he saying, Widuhar?" asked Mago.

"We are almost there—he recognises the territory. Another hour's march north and he promises we'll reach the rope bridge." Widuhar raised a cheer. "Can you hear them, shepherds, over the hill—the Golden Banners flapping in the wind? Then with my legions, and the Banners flying, we shall crush the Parthians like the winepress crushes the grape."

Because the terrain was at this point open on all sides, while farther down rocks closed threateningly in on the track, Mago decided on an immediate encampment. "If the bandits are planning to ambush us, it will be at the rope bridge. We must cross by night."

"What do we do if they cut the bridge down?" Thyrsis wanted to know.

Mago shook his head. "The bridge is as important to the bandits as it is to us. We shall erect our tents and light our fires as usual. The sky threatens snow, therefore we can expect total darkness when we come to move."

His instructions were that Thyrsis should lead an advance party, with Haji to guide them, to the bridge. "To ambush the ambushers is our only chance."

"Please let me go too, Uncle," begged Cerdic.

"You'll have important duties in camp, my boy."

"Why is it always me who's got to stay behind?" Cerdic had felt depressed all day, caged, and not a little sorry for himself. "I'm sick of just sticking up tents and pulling them down . . . You think all I'm good for is prodding a yak along."

Mago reached out a soothing hand to his nephew, but Cerdic backed away.

"I want to go with them."

"Listen, my boy! I care too much for you to deny you privileges, but this is work for those who can wield a sword. Your gift is to mend a wound, not deliver it. Be true to yourself."

"If you'd taught me how to use a sword I could've been as good a soldier as anybody."

Mago sighed. "I taught you only what I knew."

"'T' Master's right, Cerdic," came in Silenos. "There'll be need of good bandagin' if them bandits is as fierce as t'village folks says they are."

Shortly afterwards, as the tents were being erected, Cerdic got himself into another quarrel, this time with Festus. The Roman had also been gloomy all day. "Bad omens, bad omens!" he had said over and over again. "Ever since we saw that black raven, there've been signs that ill-fortune awaits us."

Cerdic had been anxiously scanning the lonely ridges. "You Romans!" he responded. "You think of nothing but bad omens. Good fortune, bad fortune . . . the gods are pleased, the gods are displeased—it's all silly nonsense! Uncle says that the Romans are the most superstitious people he's ever met."

"I don't want to hear what your uncle says," snapped back Festus.

"It's true all the same! Overturn a table—it's bad luck. Leave your dinner before it's finished—bad luck. Eat with your left hand—bad luck. Sneeze over your pudding and—"

"Shut up!" Festus brushed his red hair angrily from his eyes. "You're nothing but a Carthaginian, a barbarian—and what do barbarians understand of Roman beliefs?"

Stung to fury, Cerdic began a mocking dance. "Romans, Romans!" he chanted. "Believe in crackpot omens!" He gasped as Festus' own rage turned to blows.

One fist struck Cerdic in the pit of the stomach, another landed below his left eye. That he had never before struck a blow in anger, did not make him hesitate now. He was not himself. An inner demon had become master.

He sent a swinging fist at Festus' face. It exploded on his nose and made him roar like a lion impaled with spears.

As suddenly as it had mastered him, Cerdic's demon abandoned him. He was amazed at what he had done, full of remorse, hardly believing that the blood which gushed from Festus' nose was his doing. Then another demon got hold of him, the imp of panic. It was in Cerdic's legs, driving them into motion.

He was running, and Festus was coming after him. Away across the open grassland they went. Cerdic skirted some rocks, leapt others. Festus shouted after him, but he did not hear. He was remembering how Festus had dealt with the young Parthian. The sharp wind, and his own pace, had caused tears to almost blind Cerdic. He could hardly see the way ahead of him, though he could imagine easily enough the body of the young Parthian lying in the sand, the blood seeping through his white, shiny tunic.

In his haste, Cerdic did not notice that there were droplets of water on the wind. He was too concerned with thoughts of his pursuer. The ground had risen; there was little grass, only boulders merging into greater rock formations. The droplets on the wind were more insistent. Still they told Cerdic nothing, while the pounding of his feet and heart and the shouts of Festus muffled the sounds which came from ahead—of the river crashing through the gorge.

"Cerdic, stop!" yelled Festus in terror.

It was too late. Cerdic flew on. All at once his feet were no longer on solid ground. The earth crumbled beneath him. He was going down.

The slope was not sheer, yet it was steep, and covered with a loose carpet of pebble scree. He was skating. The pebbles churned at his feet.

The entire side of the slope was moving, touched off by the impact of Cerdic's fall. He was up to his knees in the scree, part of its motion.

Now he looked. He had gone over the edge of the gorge at a place where the cliff side had been eroded, but his journey into the cauldron below was to be no less sure.

The scree was rolling him over, covering him. It would suffocate him. He called out. All he could hear was falling stone and the boom of captive waters.

He put out his arms—and there was only space.

*　　*　　*

Bandits

As if in mourning, the afternoon skies grew dark. They opened up and swept the land with rain. Icy rain that thickened into hail, hammering against rocks, turning shale into mud. Then came the snow, soft, gentle, peace-making. And whilst the snowfall lasted, an uncanny stillness ruled the world.

6

Mago's secret weapon

He was trapped. Pains shot down his arms and legs. His head was a boulder straining his neck to breaking-point. But his brain knew only the pain of being trapped. He was in the dark, yet in a false dark, and he could hardly breath. He tried to shift his position. He was held, encased—in a sack, was it?

Hands lifted him as easily as firewood. He was against a shoulder, broad, bony, that dug into his stomach. What was this roaring sound in his ears? For a moment, his body went slack as though he had passed once more into unconsciousness. Only his brain burst with tensions: the sound was of the gorge, far louder than he had ever heard it before.

Suddenly he missed the even beat of his captor's footsteps. There was hesitation. He was swaying. It was like stepping into a boat. The roar of the gorge now threatened even to drown his thoughts.

Cerdic knew that no boat would survive three seconds in the boiling rapids. "Then they're taking me over the bridge!" A worse thought blazed through his mind. "They're going to kill me—throw me into the gorge!"

Despite his pains, his bruises, his dizziness, Cerdic fought. He rammed his knees into his captor's back. He elbowed him in the face.

Taken by surprise, the bandit lost balance and collapsed

against the rope rail. "Let me go!" screamed Cerdic. He was all arms and legs, fending off the hands which endeavoured to grasp him again.

The bridge was swaying sickeningly. Strange, he thought, that his captor had emitted no sound, did not threaten him or call for help. Faintly, Cerdic could hear voices. He had managed to wrench his head free. In the darkness, he saw hands, he saw that he lay within inches of toppling into the gorge. Those hands were going to push him over. He kicked out. He hit his captor full in the face.

He was up, and then he gasped.

"Cerdic, for the sake of the gods—stop!" The voice was that of Festus, a few strides behind him.

The young Carthaginian now realised, now saw, what he had done. "Oh Tryphon! . . ." He scrambled forward on his knees. Tryphon had dropped through the ropes and was hanging below the bridge.

Cerdic's pains were forgotten. He lay flat across the bridge. He thrust his hands under Tryphon's armpits. The waters were hissing for their prey.

He held on. He felt his own arms being tugged from their sockets. Then Festus and Thyrsis were beside him. Together, they heaved dumb Tryphon to safety.

Cerdic was desperate to explain. Tryphon merely rubbed his cheek and grinned. He ran his hand through Cerdic's hair.

"I thought—"

"Not a word!" whispered Festus, signalling Cerdic to follow him. "Remember the bandits! And cheer up—all's well!"

For two hours the caravan proceeded in silence, upwards from the gorge through wind-haunted ravines, then into open country crisp with snow. Cerdic had plenty of time to dwell on his recent misconduct. Yet he was puzzled. "I've behaved like a pig to everybody," he thought, "but nobody seems to be angry with me."

At last Mago called a brief halt. He had scarcely dismounted from his yak before Cerdic rushed at him and threw his arms around him. "Oh, Uncle! I'm worse than a rat in a sewer."

Mago hugged the boy tightly. "You fought to save yourself, what was wrong with that? After your fall, we put you in a sleeping bag to keep warm on the night journey. But I'm kicking myself for failing to take into account that poor Tryphon would be unable to answer you, reassure you, when you revived."

"How about this nephew of yours, Mago?" called Festus, his expression showing that all was forgiven. "He jumps down a mountain and is nearly washed to kingdom come—and all he can do to reward his rescuers is sleep through their hour of glory." He laid his hand proudly on his sword. "Three of us against six, Cerdic—and only one escaped us!"

"Aye," came in Thyrsis, "but that one'll stir up the hornets' nest. They'll be hot footing after us already."

As the caravan was set in motion again, Mago explained to Cerdic that they were making for a stone-built fortress at the neck of the valley. "Haji told us about it. For generations it's been abandoned, but it offers us our only chance of defence."

"I'm for marching on," said Thyrsis, "so we'll shake the bandits off altogether."

"I wish that were possible, Thyrsis. But we would be risking massacre if we did. Beyond the fort, we must pass through a narrow valley. Haji says it is a full day's journey and the bandits could attack even an army from the overhanging crags, and be confident of victory."

"Are we to stand and die?"

76

Mago's secret weapon

"A fortress such as the one Haji describes is worth twenty men. We must put our faith in its stone walls and perhaps one of my little devices . . . Keep close, everyone, we do not want to be delayed rescuing our yaks from snowdrifts. March!"

The caravan welcomed the first rays of dawn. Tides of rose-tinctured light flowed from behind the mountain ahead. Cerdic's hands and feet were numb with cold. His belly cried out for food. An inner voice told him how beautiful the morning was, but he ignored it. His eyes refused to drink in the glistening snowscape that spread outwards like precious metal and slid to the faraway gorge.

He let go a hoarse cheer when Haji identified the fort, still wrapped in shadow. Low, rough-hewn walls extended from the mountain.

"Some fort!" exclaimed Thyrsis. "Why, it's no more than a shepherd's hut!" He grunted. "You couldn't even call it a stockade."

It was indeed an uninspiring stronghold, better fitted to withstand snowstorms than the onslaught of bandits. Yet the walls were solid. They commanded trenches right round the perimeter of the fort, giving them twice their apparent height.

There was a single, thick-walled room, with look-out and firing holes.

While Silenos got a fire going and began to fry strips of dough in oil for the famished caravan, Mago surveyed the walls. "Haji says the bandits hunt in packs of thirty or more, sometimes fifty or sixty." He shook his head ruefully. "Our own army comprises but seven, if we count Haji—and that includes a half-blind old man, a boy, a madman and a cook used only to wielding pots and pans! We make a poor garrison, for we can't expect the carriers to help fight our battles."

"What's this 'device' you mentioned, Master?" inquired Thyrsis.

Mago plucked mysteriously at his beard. "In good time, Thyrsis . . . Now, Cerdic, describe the terrain to me, for that alone might be our salvation."

Cerdic noted the landscape carefully before he spoke. "The track runs down to our right almost under the shadow of the mountain. On our left the ground is more open, though the snow looks every bit as deep."

"And the mountain itself?"

"It's rounded, and overhanging, like the crust of a loaf."

"Good! That is what I had anticipated. Thyrsis, my friend, you are in command of the defences, with Festus and Tryphon to assist you." He found time to smile. "Request the aid of our Prince of Persepolis, should you need it. His legions could make all the difference to our enterprise!"

A shout came from Silenos inside the stone hut: "'Ere everybody! Get an eyeful o' this! Would you ever!" Silenos stumped out into the open, his great arms waving in excitement. "There's writin', Master . . . Writin' on t'walls! Serve me thumbs fer supper if them Romans 'aven't bin 'ere!"

The others pressed eagerly into the hut. "Over on t'far wall. Gossipy stuff, like you'd find in t'back streets o' Carthage itself."

There, in bold, crude lettering, was the second clue the caravan had found to the existence of the lost Romans:
CRASSUS PROMISED GLORY—AND WE ARE STILL WAITING.

Underneath, in almost a scribble, was added:
BEWARE OF BANDITS!

While in even smaller script was written:
AND LICE.

"Lost these Romans might have been," commented Mago, "but from this we can conclude they retained their good spirits . . . It is obvious there are no historians among them or they would have put these walls to greater use. Not a date, not a name!"

"But they came this way," said Festus, thrilled. "That's what counts!"

"I thinks I know what they mean about them lice," muttered Silenos. "I'm itchin' an' scratchin' already."

Thyrsis had been outside and now returned. "I can't find Widuhar. Has anyone seen him?"

There was to be no time to search for him. A warning shout came from Haji at the walls. The defenders streamed into the icy air. He was pointing fearfully down the valley.

Cerdic had hoped that the bandits were just a nightmare, that they existed only in the tales villagers told around their winter fires. But the bandits had stepped out of their story. At first black dots in the sun-sparkling snow, they were drawing closer and closer.

"Still a mile off," estimated Festus.

Cerdic cursed. He had counted thirty-six bandits. It couldn't be that many! He counted again—thirty-six, moving in single-file, far more swiftly than the caravan had done.

"In half an hour they'll be upon us," said Thyrsis.

Mago asked Cerdic to fetch his Bag of Tricks. "And then I want you to lead me somewhere—up into the snow." He refused to say further what his plan was. He quickly found what he required in his Bag. He wrapped various objects in sacking. "Right, Cerdic, my boy? Are you ready to be an old man's eyes?"

Together, in silence, Thyrsis and Festus waited on the wall, their swords drawn. There was Silenos too, and Tryphon—but no sign of Widuhar. The carriers had reluctantly agreed to bear arms and stood nervously back from the wall, each holding a javelin.

"What wi'lice in me pants an' shivers down me spine," complained Silenos "I'm in no fit state fer fightin'."

"Quiet!" ordered Thyrsis. He had been following the diminishing figures of Mago and Cerdic as they strode towards the dark under-face of the mountain. Beneath the "loafcrust", as Cerdic had described it, there seemed to be a passageway.

Mago and Cerdic disappeared from view.

They were, Festus calculated, almost as far away from the fort as the advancing bandits. "Coming up from behind won't help," he murmured. "Not with two of them." He sighed. "We could do with the assistance of Hannibal's Leg when the attack begins."

The bandits slowed their pace. Their leader had ordered half of them to approach the fort from the mountain side. The rest fanned out from the track, delayed but not halted by the deep snow.

"What's t'Master up to?" moaned Silenos, unable to keep quiet. "They're stalkin' up our very noses an' nothin's 'appened!"

Thyrsis did not reply. Festus glanced at him. For a man so argumentative, so contrary, in the face of battle he was wondrously calm.

Festus turned to Tryphon, "If I should die, Tryphon my friend, and you survive—will you go on to seek my father Marinius? I'm convinced he lives, and my only wish is that he should know I searched for him."

Silenos was the first to spot Widuhar. "The gods take 'im!" He pointed up the mountain, "This time 'e's skipped clean out

o'is wits like a flea from 'ot water. Our Prince is climbin'
straight fer t'summit!"

Oblivious to the petty squabbles of shepherds and bandits,
Widuhar the Immortal was racing up the giddy slopes of a
glacier as nimbly as a mountain goat.

"It's them banners 'e's after. 'E's probably shoutin' fer
t'great door in t'mountain to open up and let 'im in!"

The bandits had stopped, still five or six hundred yards
away. The sun touched their sharp-glinting spears. The
moment had come.

Suddenly there was a flash of scarlet flame to the right of the
fort. A powerful bang followed. Festus saw sparks, then
another flame. There was a second bang.

In amazement, the bandits wheeled round. But neither the
flashes nor the bangs were enough to persuade them to retreat.
They stood firm.

"It's failed," Festus decided. "They're coming on!"

What happened next forced Festus to take back his words.
The whole mountain had begun to shudder. The gigantic crust
of snow was rent by cracks which darted like black lightning to
the summit. A dull, faraway rumble grew into a thunderous
roar. The head of the mountain was sliding forward into the
valley, layer upon layer of rolling snow building up from
pressures above and being thrust on at a devastating speed.

Snow clouds burst out into the blue air, choking the sunlight. All who watched remained rock-still in fascination and
horror. The avalance seemed about to destroy every visible
thing.

"It's th'end o't'world!" wailed Silenos.

Jagged slabs of ice spun out of the mist of powdery snow.
The roar advanced, drowning the pitiful screams of the bandits. They ran, leaping through the snow, casting away their

arms, glancing over their shoulders at the breakers of ice and snow that swept onwards, overwhelmingly, higher and more powerfully than any sea-storm imaginable.

One moment they were racing before the billowing white mist, the next they were gone.

The mountain's anger at being shaken from winter sleep continued for several minutes. Then, slowly, the force of the avalanche ebbed away. The valley no longer existed in its former shape; only time, sunlight and spring warmth would restore its identity.

"Here they come!" Thyrsis led the chorus of cheers which greeted the explorer as he returned, steadied by Cerdic. "Was there ever magic like Mago's?"

On reaching the fortress wall, Mago stayed, breathless. He shaded his weak eyes and for many moments stared at his handiwork. He did not speak. He lowered his head. There was no glint of celebration in his expression. "I take no delight in this destruction," he said, bitterness in his voice. "My mission has been to discover and preserve life, and my inventions have always been in the service of man. This time the alternative was to see those about me die. May the gods pardon me!"

"May they honour and bless you!" affirmed Thyrsis. "With such a weapon, Master, who knows what glory Carthage could win for herself?"

Mago replied gravely. "The weapon is buried beneath the mountain. And its secret too is buried. Speak no more of it."

Festus came running from the far side of the fort. He had stayed, after greeting Mago and Cerdic, scanning what was left of the mountain. "Mago! Widuhar was up there when—when it happened. He's vanished!"

At first Mago refused to believe it. "I left orders—that no one should move from within the walls. At his peril! Then fetch the spades. Muster the carriers—everyone!" He asked Festus to think carefully where he remembered seeing Widuhar. "If he got as far as the snow crust—"

"That's where he was heading. But he was only on the lower reaches. At the very edge of the crust."

"There's hope, then." The entire caravan, save for one carrier who remained to look after the animals, raced out into the snow. Part of the avalanche had spread as far as the slope below the fort. It had been waist deep in places; now it was more than head high, and a way had to be dug through.

"If Widuhar's under all this lot, Master," Silenos wanted to know, "will 'e not 'ave suffoclated?"

A laugh went up from the diggers.

"Suffoclated, Silenos? No . . . He might survive an hour, perhaps more, if he could have found himself a pocket of air and kept his arm against his face."

They were directly under the spot identified by Festus. "Dig!" ordered Mago. "With all your strength."

The sun climbed to the pinnacle of the sky. The digging continued, revealing nothing. The sun tilted on its axis towards the west. There was to be no respite for the labourers in the snow. Thirst was quenched by handfuls of snow. Sweat was doused by it, and still the gleaming white terrain gave no sign of delivering up its captive.

Then, from Cerdic, came a yelp of joy. He had wandered off to dig a hole of his own. "A boot!" he cried. "Quick, everybody!" The diggers converged, but stood back for Mago.

"That's Widuhar all right. Extreme care, now."

Cerdic, Festus and Thyrsis concentrated on the "head end" while Tryphon and Silenos battled away to find another boot, another leg.

"We're nearly there!" shouted Festus. "Oh let him be

alive!" Their hands were red and aching terribly with the cold; but they hardly noticed.

"He's twisted over," said Thyrsis. Gradually the snow-dungeon of the Prince of Persepolis was scratched away. Every face stared down as Festus slipped his hands under Widuhar's head and eased it clear of the snow.

The eyes opened. There was a cheer almost loud enough to bring down another avalanche. Widuhar stared at his rescuers. His mouth opened:

"My people!" he whispered. He struggled to raise himself. "I saw them—the Banners! The Banners were in my grasp . . . I tracked the Host to their mountain home . . . Their footsteps were in the snow!"

"Lift him gently," commanded Mago. "Wrap him in my cloak."

"The great door of the mountain suddenly opened up to me, I, Prince of—"

"Here, Prince," said Thyrsis, gripping Widuhar tightly, "Drink this wine-spirit. It'll put those Banners out of mind for a while."

"I saw them! At the head of the Host."

Widuhar was carried out of the snow, still babbling of banners and gold, of armies on the march and the once-and-for-ever defeat of the Parthians.

"Do you hear, Silenos?" Mago called. "Hot broth for him—and for all of us."

"And don't forget the salt!" reminded Cerdic.

7

The desert trail

Because Mago's fast-fading eyesight had begun to prevent him writing up his Log of the journey, the duty of scribe fell to Cerdic. Each evening, in the restful twilight, Mago would dictate and Cerdic would write, sometimes reminding his uncle of things he had forgotten—such as the hunting incident when a mischievous ghost robbed the caravan of a feast.

"The heart of winter has slowly melted into spring," stated Mago's Log, "and we have descended from the Roof of the World, as the local people call it, through monotonous vistas of rock and desolate, wind-eroded plains. Our supplies of food became so low that we were reduced to a once-daily diet of dried beans and dough-strips fried in oil. Poor Silenos ran out of salt!

"Then, on the slopes of a forested valley, we spotted antelope. What a feast we imagined ahead of us! Off went Cerdic and Festus with bow and javelin. Their patience in stalking the beasts was remarkable. Yet, on every single occasion when they took aim, something disturbed the prey.

"Either those antelope had the power to see through rocks or there was trickery at work, human or divine. Our young hunters turned their attention from the antelope to what they suspected was the phantom of the rocks. They had observed

85

that, each time the animals bolted, there was a crack of pebbles, as if the wind herself were casting stones.

"An ambush was duly prepared by the hunters. After tracking an antelope for a whole afternoon, they hid behind rocks as usual. They took aim but instead of letting fly another fruitless arrow, they sprinted round the rocks, Cerdic one way, Festus the other—to discover Haji, our guide, squatting before his tell-tale pile of stones.

"All is now forgiven, despite our stomachs continuing empty of meat. It seems Haji was not merely causing mischief. He was protecting his ancestors! The mountain folk believe the spirits of their dead enter the bodies of certain animals. They take refuge there before passing on to the heavenly kingdom. To kill such a beast is to rob the dead of the chance of paradise. Our own loss is thus nothing in comparison!"

The Log of a few days later told of happier prospects:

"We have left behind us the arid wilderness and entered a land of fertile valleys. The fields are thick with grass and traversed by wide rivers, whose waters are delicious to drink and full of fish. I have gathered specimens of white jonquil, irises of vibrant purple and a species of orchid, stringy-tailed like a lizard. I have also caught many rare butterflies and other insects such as the grasshopper, which the village children keep in little wooden cages hung with bells.

"The houses in the villages are built of mud-brick and wood, with a hole through the roof to let out the smoke of open-hearth fires. The people are gentle and hospitable, and for the first time in weeks we have eaten well—of roasted lamb, fresh trout and the earth apple which is as tasty whether it is boiled, roasted or fried.

"The villagers can hardly believe we have crossed the Roof of the World. They say that only once before, years and years ago, did men of light skins descend from the mountains. Yet again we are in the footprints of the Romans!

"They are spoken of as the Square Arms. I take this to be a reference to the scutum, the Roman shield, curved to the shape of the body and squared off at top and bottom.

"When we ask how many years have passed since the Square Arms marched this way, the villagers shake their heads. What is a year? They do not measure time as we do. Nor can they tell us what fate befell the Square Arms. They point eastwards to the desert, which we shall soon be reaching.

"None survives the Great Desert, they say, for if a traveller does not die of thirst or starvation, or go mad in the heat of the sun, he falls a victim of the warriors of the Fire King, who lives beyond the desert. If there is but a grain of truth in the tales the villagers tell of the Fire King, then he is truly a monster. They claim he drinks the blood of the slain. And he is the mortal enemy of the Seres.

"Yes, at last, we have found people who speak of the Land Beyond the North Wind, the country of the Seres. None has ever been there but some claim to remember Seric merchants passing this way before the Fire King cut off the westward trade routes.

"The ruler of the Seres is called the Emperor of Heaven. The villagers have heard that he possesses a whip which can remove mountains and halt the flow of rivers; a spade that by itself can dig a third of a mile a day, and a flying horse capable of galloping a thousand miles between dawn and sunset. When it stamps its foot, they say, a tower springs up . . .

"Doubtless in time they will speak of our portly Silenos as having been twice the weight of a hundred sheep, and my black beard as being so long it took ten men to carry it!"

No gift—save for his harp—had ever delighted Cerdic more

than the horse he now rode. Mago had bartered for it, and another for Festus, with tumblers of glass, gems of red coral and rolls of thin-spun cloth. The villagers called them "Blood Sweaters" for, they claimed, when the horses were galloped long and hard they began to sweat blood at the neck.

The Fire King rode them, and his people, the Hsiung-nu. They were bred in Farghana in distant Badakshan and Cerdic and Festus were told how, centuries before, the Emperor of Heaven sent an army to obtain horses from Farghana. But the cruel desert in winter, and many misfortunes, brought disaster to the expedition. A whole army was lost merely to bring back a few precious horses.

Cerdic had named his horse Pytheus, after the explorer who Mago believed to be the most distinguished of all travellers into the unknown, and who had been the first to map the shores of that northern island called Pretain.

How hot, how dry, the wind is, thought Cerdic as he raced with Festus along a willow-lined river. The landscape was a blur. Green merged with blue-reflecting waters and globes of yellow fire floated into the corners of his eyes from the river banks. Then, between the shoulders of the hills, emerged another fire, red now, as though the sun had come crashing down before its time.

"Look, Festus! The desert!"

They rode to the crest of the highest hill in a bare range— gateway to a vast ocean of sand. They dismounted. They stood in awe at the vision before them. The dazzling yellow of the dunes in the foreground rippled into shades of orange, then passed into a fiery distance. The wind had hewn the desert into shadowy ridges like gigantic waves frozen in motion; and above everything was a shimmering veil of golden light.

"We'll miss Haji," said Cerdic, turning to watch the caravan winding through the sandhills. "He spoiled our feast but he was a good guide. When he gets home with his pay he's going to buy a flock of sheep—and a wife!"

"We'll also miss our faithful carriers," replied Festus. "I don't care for the new guide, Mujid. He's shifty-eyed."

"Uncle's not happy with him either. But Mujid knows the desert. And he's the only one who didn't spit on our money."

"Yes, and the carriers he's hired look a real bunch of cut-throats."

"True, but the camels' humps are in the right place, and they've all got four legs. I counted them myself!"

Festus remained uneasy. "Just the same, Mujid thinks we're madmen to risk both the desert and the horsemen of the Fire King." He stared out to where crimson sun and crimson desert would soon collide. "And but for the thought that my father lives somewhere beyond all that, I'd think we were madmen too."

The caravan had slowed to a halt. Mago had been helped from his camel by Tryphon. He was approaching Thyrsis who beckoned to him excitedly.

"What's he pointing at, can you see?"

Festus answered by mounting his horse. "Come on, Thyrsis doesn't get excited for nothing."

Spreading dust clouds behind them, the two friends galloped towards the caravan. Thyrsis' discovery had caused considerable mirth.

"Another cairn of stones!" observed Cerdic as they reached the level track.

"But there's more. What is it, Thyrsis?" called Festus.

Thyrsis held up a wooden pole which had been sticking up from the cairn. In his other hand was a piece of carving, badly weathered, but recognisable as a ship. "She's a Roman galley! And see what's written."

Festus took the ship. He turned it in the sunlight. Along the hull, the inscription stated simply:

"ROMA, 2000 Miles."

"Pointing due west," grinned Thyrsis.

"If that's really 'ow far we've come," declared Silenos, "we'll not get back 'afore our Cerdic's lost 'is teeth an' 'is 'air's turned grey!"

"But why?" Festus wanted to know. "Why all this far? Why risk death in the desert—and then leave nothing but a sign-post?"

Mago agreed that for so many men to hazard the desert crossing, probably not knowing how far it was, how long it would take and whether the few oases would be able to provide enough food and water, appeared to be foolhardy madness.

Originally he had attempted to explain the eastward journey of the Romans—if they really were Romans—as following in the steps of the great expedition of Alexander. This, having plunged farther east than any in recorded history, veered south down the valley of the Indus River to the Erithraean Sea. "Then they would find ships to sail them home. Yet if such had been the Roman's intention they would have turned south long before now."

"Could they just have got lost, Uncle?" Cerdic asked.

"It's more likely, I'm beginning to think, that they travelled east under compulsion."

"As prisoners?"

"Either that, or they had no intention of returning home."

"Impossible!" cried Festus. "Every Roman loves his homeland. And how could anyone prefer this wilderness to the beauty and comfort of Italy?"

"Tell me, Festus, how old are you?"

"Eighteen—nearly."

"Yes, and it is almost that long since the Battle of Carrhae. Eighteen years! Many of them will scarcely remember Rome. They are soldiers and will have fought many battles since then. If they have grown used to such a life, they will have accepted it as their fate . . . I beg you, Festus, should we ever come upon the Host, and find your father, do not expect too much of him."

Festus nodded. He accepted this advice. "But do you really think they are prisoners, Mago, slaves once more?"

Mago held his hand out for the model ship. "No. This was carved by a knife and at leisure; slaves are permitted neither knives nor leisure. The explanation must lie elsewhere."

If, in his travels with Mago, Cerdic had often missed the delight of playing games, there was to be time in the desert to make up for the loss. Games! With words and with numbers, games of observation and memory; new games, old games, sitting games, standing games—anything to defeat the tedium of the long days of marching through the endless vistas of sand. Between them, Cerdic and Festus invented twenty new games in a single day. They composed songs which Cerdic accompanied on his harp—songs that reflected the constant thoughts, and indeed dreams, of the caravan: of food, tables heavy-laden with it, beautiful, wonderful, tasty, tender—food! In the hot blue air Cerdic began to see visions of it as Pytheus tramped hour after weary hour across the flat wastes. Veal pasties seemed to sprout up through the golden sand; every stone was a mellon, every withered root a tree flourishing with oranges, pears and apricots.

Even Mago, whose mind was usually occupied with greater matters than the sustenance of the stomach, allowed himself to reflect upon memories of better eating days. "I met your great Roman orator, Cicero, some years ago," he told Festus, "and he had strong opinions on what should make up a civilised feast. His favourite dish was flesh of saltfish cooked in oil, filleted and mixed with brains, poultry liver, hard-boiled eggs and cheese. The whole was then cooked over a slow fire after being sprinkled with a sauce of pounded pepper, lovage—I think he said—marjoram, rueberries, honey and oil. Delicious, wouldn't you say?"

The evenings were best, when Cerdic played the harp, feeling the sharp desert wind on his back and the warm glow of the campfire on his face; and when Mago told tales of his adventures. "Did I ever tell you . . . ?" he would begin, and Cerdic's exhaustion would be forgotten as he listened to his uncle describing the famous basilisk in Africa, the half-upright monster which breathed poisonous gas, fatal to all creatures, and which dissolved at cockcrow; or the people called "Shady Feet" who, it was claimed, had feet so large that their owners used them as sunshades when they lay on their backs.

Cerdic's favourite of the many tales the villagers had told of the People Beyond the North Wind was of an emperor's love for a princess who never smiled. All the poor monarch's efforts to make her smile failed. Jugglers, clowns, story-tellers—none could ever change her doleful expression. Now the emperor was threatened by foreign invaders and he had set beacons on every high hill in his empire. In the hope that he would make her smile, he set all the beacons alight. And still she did not smile.

Yet, when the foreign soldiers did invade, the people thought their emperor was at his jokes again; they ignored the beacons and did not prepare to defend themselves. At last the princess smiled! And she laughed when the invaders attacked the emperor's capital and cut off his head. Thus the saying had grown up, "The smile of a beauty overturned an empire".

During the breathless heat of the day, each traveller kept to his own thoughts. For Silenos, though, to think was to speak and to speak was to talk of home, and of his happy years in the service of Mago. "There'd 'ave bin none o' this travellin' up 'ill, down dale an' round the 'ouses," he told Festus, "if t'Master's wife'd lived. A rare young beauty she was—died o't'fever not twelve months after t' weddin'. Eyes like bright sapphires she 'ad. And could she sing! Sweet as a lark, soft as a dove, t'Master used to say . . . You can still feel 'er on Mago's isle. She'll be lookin' after things till we gets back.

"And what things to be lookin' after! Books, y've never seen so many. T'library at Alexander's a brush-cupboard in comparison. Animals livin', animals dead, 'e's got 'em, and some 'e says died out millions o' years since—'e's got skeletons of them, monsters wi' tails the length o' three camels stood end to end, six-inch long teeth and spikes down their backs . . . Then there's 'is birds and 'is plants and 'is rocks and 'is fossules. Aye . . . " His voice would become sad. "An 'ouse full o' things to replace 'er as was lost."

The second week of the caravan's desert journey closed joyfully with the location of an oasis. A clear, deep pool, fed by an underground stream, was surrounded by palms and willows. Bright-winged insects hovered between sunlight and shadow and the air was perfumed by fragrant tamarisks, hardy shrubs with blossoms of radiant pink.

Since then there had been little joy. Another five days had passed and spirits were low. Silenos' food grew sparser in quantity, less nourishing: balls of dough sprinkled meagrely

93

with seasoning, followed by dates or a small handful of currants.

The water-supply had to be rationed to half a cup twice a day for each member of the caravan. There was less comradely talk, more snapping comments as the sun's heat seemed to become more intense as the journey progressed.

The attitude of Mujid, the guide, and the carriers, was Mago's chief problem. They did not want to go on. Their fear increased, visibly, from day to day. They were racked with superstitions. One night when a yak wandered from the encampment and fell into a trench made by a former caravan in search of water, there was unanimous agreement that the spirits of the desert were angry. They had sent an ill-omen.

The carriers became fiercely quarrelsome. Mujid made no attempt to control them. Nothing but misfortune lay ahead of the caravan, he declared. He was slow to pass on orders and the carriers were slow to obey them, and then only sullenly, mutteringly.

After a long day's march they would huddle together in the dark, arguing among themselves, calling across the camp, and pointing accusing fingers at Mago.

There was evidence, too, of theft. Each morning the flasks contained less water than the night before. Mago was obliged to mount a constant guard over both the water and other supplies.

"We shall have a rebellion on our hands before very long," believed Thyrsis, and no one felt confident enough to disagree with him.

"That Mujid'll 'ave me ladle down 'is throat if 'e yatters on about t' food much more," said Silenos.

It was difficult in the mornings to get the carriers to load up. They deliberately wasted time, roping the animals so that the packs would slip off as soon as the caravan was ordered forward. They insisted on long rests in the middle of the day but refused to take a step farther when the sun fell below the horizon, though there might be an hour of daylight left. They protested against the growing desert heat; they protested against the bitter cold of night.

The slightest accident, the slightest divergence from the monotonous daily ritual, was interpreted as an evil sign. The bones of a camel or a yak abandoned in the sand were enough to halt the caravan for a full day. Only after offers of higher wages, and hours of heated argument, could the journey continue.

Then came the unfortunate discovery of human bones, scattered by the desert wind across the caravan's track. Flies hummed in black clusters around the skull that gleamed in the light, and made the carriers shrink back in horror.

Mago tried to reassure them, bring them to order. But Mujid refused to translate. Instead, he roared accusations at Mago. This was the end of the journey. "We go!" he cried. He turned. He shouted at the carriers. They wheeled their beasts round.

"Wait!" appealed Mago.

He was ignored. "We go!" repeated Mujid bluntly.

"But not with our stores—"

"You return with us. We go! Now!"

There was silence. All eyes were on Mago, while the yaks were already nodding their lazy heads towards the west.

"Have we come this far," said Mago solemnly, "suffered so many dangers, driven ourselves over mountain passes, through drifts of snow that reached to our very necks, fought off bandits and negotiated the very Roof of the World, to be driven from our course by one human skeleton? Have I lost

95

everything from my eyes but shadows, to turn back when the distance we have come might well be more than that we have to travel? Never!"

"Never!" roared Widuhar in support. "The Banners lie east—my messengers tell me so."

Mujid waited no longer. He issued a sharp command. Every pack animal was to head west, and the moment his order had been given, the carriers began to run, tugging the yaks, and four of the camels, behind them.

Acting on his own initiative, Thyrsis urged his camel in pursuit. He had drawn a javelin from his pack. With a piercing war cry he drove in among the carriers. But their fear of the desert spirits was greater than Thyrsis' threats—until those threats were carried out.

He hurled his javelin at the leading deserter. Its force pinioned him to the sand. "How many more?" shouted Thyrsis, rounding on the carriers who had stopped in their tracks. "How many more skeletons?"

They understood. Their fear of Thyrsis was, for the moment at least, greater than their fear of the desert spirits.

A groan of dismay came from Mago when he realised what Thyrsis had done. He dismounted. He crossed to where the dead carrier lay, and knelt beside him. "He committed no crime, and my ambition has been the death of him." For the first time on the expedition, Mago's resolution left him. "My friends," he called in a broken voice, "decide what you will . . ."

Cerdic's shadow fell across his uncle. He had never seen him like this before, so robbed of certainty. "We must bury him, Uncle," he said. "And then we must be on our way."

"West, my boy?"

"And make Thyrsis feel he's killed a man for no reason

at all? East and east and east, Uncle—that's what you told us!"

"I go east to find my father," came in Festus. "Force me to return and my own bones will lie in the desert."

The caravan marched on, veering northwards for two days to what Mujid said was the only water hole within a hundred miles. Cerdic's throat had swelled so that he could hardly swallow; his mouth felt as though he had chewed dried leaves. He had developed a hacking cough which made his mouth drier and his throat painfully sore. The flesh around his eyes was puffed up. His skin had peeled and itched violently. Each morning, the moment he mounted his horse, he felt the strength given him by sleep drain straight out of him into the sand.

Mago had demanded no tasks of him but one: to play the harp. "All I request of you, Cerdic," he had said, "is to soothe our troubled hearts with your music." And in playing, Cerdic knew that he had something to contribute to the survival of his comrades.

The harp's song gave the travellers back their dreams, and in their dreams was hope. It seemed to defy the immensity of the desert, for it lifted the minds of the silent listeners out of this crushing desolation, and by doing so, lessened its power over them.

In the daylight, a desert of sand, in darkness a black desert of stars—both infinitely vast, yet Cerdic's music made them shrink to an arm's length. He was back in Uncle Mago's study, surrounded by maps and charts, scientific contraptions and shelves of specimens—plants, rocks, shells, butterflies, spiders and moths. A scent of wallflowers wafted in on the sea breeze.

97

He saw Julia, Silenos' little niece, picking strawberries in the garden, framed against the lustrous silver of the sea.

But such thoughts were driven away when the caravan discovered that Mujid's waterhole had dried up. The broken walls of a former habitation rose from the drifting sand. Withered tamarisks indicated the place where the well had been.

Mujid was crouched in the hollow, his head down, waving his arms and repeating over and over, "It was here! Water! Plenty! I tell you, we cursed by desert spirits."

The other carriers were furious. Abandoning the yaks, they hurled themselves upon Mujid, screaming, and beating him with more energy than they had shown on the entire journey. Thyrsis and Festus scattered them and Mago stood over the hapless guide. "What are they chanting, Mujid?"

"About the camel."

"That we left to die yesterday? You told us that was the tradition of the desert, Mujid."

"Aye, but its spirit—bad! Came and drunk up water."

Suddenly, Widuhar, who had strayed from the halted caravan, appeared silhouetted above the high dunes. "Salvation, shepherds!" he cried. "Over there!" He pointed. "A palace, sparkling with fountains and lakes." Perhaps only in that moment of utter desperation could Widuhar have made his friends believe him. "Look!" There was a rush up the sand. "My own kingdom has risen from the desert!"

Indeed Widuhar could have been forgiven his imaginings, for in the strange, all-enveloping light that occurs when the sun is directly above, there appeared to be a whitish-blue mist across the land, and in the centre of it were shapes.

"I can see it too, by the gods!" shouted Silenos. "Towers an' things." He cheered. "And there's rivers flowin'."

The desert trail

"Gardens!" burst in Festus. "I can see gardens—trees, lawns . . ." Cerdic had led Mago to the top of the sand crest. He too was amazed. "There *are* towers, Uncle . . . It's a palace, really!"

Now everyone was cheering—save Mago. He shook his head.

"Shall I give the order to march, Master?" asked Thyrsis eagerly. "It's not a mile off."

"No, not a mile off," replied Mago, "nor a hundred miles off. Give no orders."

"But we're dying!"

"We dig. Here at the waterhole."

"I cannot understand you, Master? Dig for water when there are rivers and lakes a few minutes away?"

"Friends," announced Mago. "I have heard of such experiences as this. They are called a mirage. Exhausted travellers see them in the mist of the distance. The images are often so real to everyone who sees them, that the travellers stumble on and on, while the palaces, the rivers, edge always that little way farther off. Trust me! I tell you, in an hour's time, your palace will have vanished into dust."

Slowly, each of the members of the caravan turned to gaze upon the spectacle before them. They saw palace towers, rivers and lakes. There was silence.

"Trust me," repeated Mago.

The others relented, but not Thyrsis.

"Then take a camel, Thyrsis, and if you bring back one leaf of a tree or one drop of the crystal lake—I promise you we will follow you . . . In the meantime, we dig!"

8

Eyes without faces

Breathless even before it was his turn to dig, Cerdic joined Festus in the hole begun by Mago and Tryphon. It was now three feet deep. He worked until there was a blackness before his eyes. He felt himself swaying, but he kept on. There was purpose in this, better than watching in exasperation as dry sand merely revealed more dry sand.

"We've reached clay!" shouted Festus, pausing to wipe streams of sweat from his eyes. "Dry still, and bluish."

Four feet, five feet. The limits of Cerdic's strength had been passed long ago. Yet still he pressed the spade into the clay with his foot; still he heaved crumbling loads to the surface. Blisters had grown on his hands without him noticing them. They burst and bled. He sucked the blood, even squeezed the blisters to dampen his mouth.

Then it was the turn of Widuhar and Silenos. The fat cook was steaming as though he had walked under a shower of hot water. He did his best, but the effort proved too much for him. He collapsed in the hole and had to be hauled out. "Nothin' but rock!" he wailed in bitter disappointment.

Mago climbed into the trench which had reached eight feet. He examined the uncovered ground. What Silenos had said was true. "We'll find no water on this spot," he decided. "We must start all over again—at the roots of the tamarisks lower down."

"It impossible!" shouted Mujid. "We waste time. Got to go back—now!"

Thyrsis had returned, disconsolate. He slipped wearily from his camel. "As you said it would, Master, our palace disappeared into dust. There was nothing—nothing!"

"We leave!" repeated Mujid.

"That we cannot do, Mujid," replied Mago. He stood facing only partly in Mujid's direction, for the desert brilliance had robbed his eyes of their last power. "We would never reach the oasis alive. It is eight days' march at least. The animals have had nothing to drink for two days—just one of them could consume all the water we have left. We have sufficient for a single day. We must dig—and dig here!"

He held out the spade handle. Mujid seized it and threw it to the ground. "Not me. I return my village. You pay wages." The carriers murmured in agreement.

"You will die on the journey, Mujid."

"That better than die here, alone. The gods—angry! We go, but first give us share of food and water."

"We will dig one more pit, Mujid, then we will discuss terms."

"We no discuss!"

The carriers shouted their support: "Water! Give water!" They surged round Mago, pushing him backwards. He fell. They trampled over him in the direction of the yak bearing the last waterskins. "Stop them!" Mago cried. "Or all is lost."

Cerdic grabbed a spade. Festus was running forward, his sword raised for action. Silenos puffed heavily away to return brandishing his ladle.

But the desperate carriers had already shrunk from the point of Thyrsis' javelin. On his orders, they queued in twos to take their turn in digging the second trench.

Mujid had been felled by a blow from Hannibal's Leg. He rose, obedient for the present, but clearly determined to cause trouble again at the first opportunity. Grimly, he took back the spade. He began to dig.

The sun had tilted beyond the high dunes. Shadows lengthened across the red-glowing sand. The second trench was more than ten feet deep. The diggers were cutting through the same bluish clay. Cerdic dropped panting in the shadow of his horse, Pytheus. He felt more sorry for him than he did for himself. The creature's noble head drooped as pathetically as its tail.

Cerdic stroked the horse's muzzle. He pressed his face into its mane. "It will be all right, Pytheus," he whispered. "Soon."

His mind was in a haze, between sleep and waking. His eyes closed. His eyes opened. Something crossed his vision, at the end of his feet. Something black. It had stopped, then (was it in his dream or in his waking?) it climbed on his foot. He lay still, burningly awake.

The black scorpion was advancing down his body. He was suddenly too weak and too terrified to shake it off. It had reached his stomach. His lips opened, but he could not summon the strength to call out.

One move, he knew, and the scorpion would sting him. He would feel agony, then he would die. It was on his chest. If it came to his throat . . .

"At last!" Festus roared in triumph. "There's damp."

Cerdic jumped with fright and the scorpion, turning on its tail, scuttled off into the sand. He was on his feet, gasping with relief. "Damp, you say, Festus?"

His friend stood back in the trench, now some twelve feet

deep. The whole caravan crowded round as Festus, and Tryphon, dug with renewed energy.

Moisture began to rise through the clay. More spadefuls, and the clay was becoming mud. More spadefuls, and water began to seep into a shallow pool. More spadefuls, and there was enough to scoop up with a cup.

"Stand back!" commanded Thyrsis as the carriers began to jostle each other at the edge of the trench.

"One mouthful only, to begin with," said Mago. "Then the horses and yaks must be provided for. The camels can wait till we have drunk our fill."

So slow, so slow it seemed, to gather one cup of precious water. All eyes fixed upon the cup as Festus offered it to Tryphon who put it to his lips. All eyes drinking the water that Tryphon drank; all mouths feeling the cool liquid on the tongue, life-giving, trickling down throats of parchment. Slowly, so slowly, the cup was refilled. Festus drank his share, then one by one the members of the caravan took the cup, spilling not a drop, saying not a word.

Further digging reached a bubbling spring which, amid great rejoicing, slaked the deepest thirst and later provided for the animals.

Mujid was to destroy the brief period of happy concord between his men and Mago's. "Now we have water," he said. "We return, at once!"

Mago had been leaning on his staff. He straightened up. He reached out with Hannibal's Leg and drew two crosses in the sand. "Look, my friend. Here is our position, and there is the oasis." To the east of the caravan he inscribed a line. "This is where the desert ends, I am sure of it. Beyond, are hills and rivers and eventually, the land of the Seres. There!"

He brought the heel of Hannibal's Leg down on the map of sand. "In the name of learning, and of Carthage, we go east!"

Darkness. A quickening wind over the dunes. A night full of hollow dreams, of whispers, of spectres of bones lying on the desert wastes. How small, came the whispers, how small we are; how meaningless, each life but a flicker, visible, then gone for ever.

Cerdic awoke to the whispers, glad that it was only the murmurs of the night he was hearing, and not the angry roars of the Cyclops whose story Mago had told him by the camp fire. In his dream, Cerdic had been there, with Odysseus the wanderer, trapped in the one-eyed giant's cave, and he had seen Odysseus plunge the red-hot branch into the Cyclops' eye.

He must have cried out for Festus raised his head sharply from his own dreams. "What's wrong?"

Unwilling to confess that he had been scared by a mere dream, Cerdic said he thought he had heard something. "Probably Widuhar mumbling on about his Golden Banners."

Yet the sounds came again. Festus was suddenly alert. He shifted forward on to his knees. "Like somebody in pain. We'd better check."

Cerdic unlaced the entrance flaps of the tent while Festus belted on his sword. Together, they peered out. At first they could see only the sunken fire sending a thread of smoke into the darkness.

"Strange!" Cerdic tried to make out the familiar shapes of the animals in the shelter of a high dune. "Very strange!" Usually there was some restless movement from the yaks.

Then he gasped. He saw Pytheus roaming loose against the lightening sky. "Something terrible has happened."

Festus was already sounding the alarm. "Mago! Tryphon! Thyrsis! Wake up! Wake up, everybody!" With Cerdic behind him, he ran to where Widuhar should have been standing guard over the animals. "Gone! All of them, gone."

They raced to the top of the dune. Pytheus came trotting to Cerdic. Farther away was Festus' own horse, nibbling at a tamarisk.

Festus turned and shouted down to Mago who, guided by Tryphon, strode across the camp. "All our animals—gone! And no sign of Mujid or the carriers."

"Then they've fled westwards."

"There's one yak left," called Cerdic, spotting the beast where the sand was blackest against the approaching dawn. He ran after it. He patted its head. "So you've saved Uncle Mago's Bag of Tricks, eh? And one water skin."

Meanwhile, Festus had discovered Widuhar. The Prince of Persepolis lay groaning, half-conscious, at the bottom of the high dune. He had been badly beaten. Blood pumped from a gash above his ear. "The Parthians came at me," he panted. "Ten thousand of 'em."

"Lie still," commanded Mago. "Thyrsis, light a torch . . . Cerdic, do you hear? Come quickly."

"Is it serious?" asked Festus anxiously.

Mago traced the wound with his finger-ends. "He is in no danger, except from loss of blood." He gave a profound sigh of relief when Cerdic announced that the Bag of Tricks was safe.

"Then the gods have not deserted us entirely. Bring the Bag, Cerdic. This knife-wound will have to be stitched and you must do it."

The others stood round in awe as Cerdic made preparations. All at once, he was calm. He knew exactly what to do—and had he not practised often enough on injured animals?

He untied the leather satchel in which Mago kept his surgical instruments. With a pair of bronze tweezers he held out a long needle to Festus. "You can help," he said, "by holding the end of the needle in the flame of Thyrsis' torch, while I wash my hands at the spring."

The silver light of morning touched the desert horizon. Dew-laden, the surfaces of the dunes began to sparkle as though heaped with diamonds. Thyrsis' torch paled in the advancing light.

"All right, Uncle." Cerdic stood up. He gazed at his handiwork. "The job's done!"

"Well I never!" Silenos had come from the fire he had been rekindling. "That's as fine a bit o' stitchin' as me ol'granddam ever did!" Cerdic's ears resounded with praise. "I'll know who to come to when I wants me socks darnin' i'future!"

Mago beamed with pride. He ruffled Cerdic's hair. "Your further instructions, Master Surgeon?"

Cerdic mimed his uncle. He pretended to stroke an imaginary beard. "I'd advise a strict control on the number of Parthians he's allowed for supper."

Only now did the caravan begin to realise the consequences of Mujid's treachery. There was water enough, but the carriers had deserted with all the food stores and with the goods Mago planned to trade with the People Beyond the North Wind—rolls of purple-dyed cloth, ornaments of amber and red coral, and gifts such as rhinoceros horns, gold talismans and parchment books by the great Western philosophers such as Aristotle, Plato and Pythagoras.

"You still have your Bag of Tricks, Uncle," reminded Cerdic, "and your Log."

"But no animals," interrupted Thyrsis. "No food."

If Mago felt despair, he did not show it. "We shall load one tent on each of the Farghana horses. The yak will take another. We have legs to walk on, and I have enough gold about me to buy more animals."

"Has the sun robbed you of your wits as well as your eyes, Master?" asked Thyrsis. "We are not camels that can march for days without eating or drinking. And where shall we march? Where will we find animals to buy?" He squatted down in the sand. "We are done for. We might as well remain here and wait for death."

Mago showed neither anger nor impatience. He knelt down beside Thyrsis. "Do you remember, long ago, when by my offices you were released from the galleys? You had given up hope of ever being free again of the iron manacles and the cruel whip. You thought to kill yourself, but you took courage. You waited one more day, then another . . . So you must do now, Thyrsis. Trust me! Beyond this desert lies a great empire, greater than Rome—and we shall be the first to discover it, Mago the Carthaginian, Thyrsis of Syracuse—all of us!"

"Remember the Banners!" cried Widuhar, forgetful of his wounds. "The Golden Banners!"

Thyrsis got to his feet. "We shall die anyway, so what does it matter? Give the orders, and I shall obey them."

The tents had been packed, the camp cleared, and Mago signalled the caravan into motion.

But nobody moved. Thyrsis at the head of the caravan, Cerdic, Festus and Tryphon behind him, Silenos and Widuhar at the rear, all stared upwards as though there had been an eclipse of the sun. Yet Mago, in his blindness, remained oblivious to the spell that had been cast on them. "Why do you delay?"

Cerdic tried to answer, but he was too frightened to speak. The sun had suffered no eclipse. Rather it had been obscured by earthly shadows. Scores of them pointed downwards from the rim of the dunes.

"Horsemen, Uncle . . . Everywhere!"

It seemed that the black-clad riders who surrounded the caravan had eyes but no faces: unmoving eyes, bright as arrow-points, shining from between black masks and flowing black hoods.

They bore spears and curved swords that widened towards the point. Their tunics were of animal skins, their boots knee high and of black fur.

The only sound came from Pytheus, who whinnied at the sight of the warriors' Farghana horses.

"Be as stone, everyone!" instructed Mago. "We need not consult the Oracle to learn that we have encountered the dreaded Hsiung-nu . . . Tell me, Cerdic, is there one among them who lives in the heart of a golden flame?"

"They are all in black, Uncle."

"Then the Fire King is not with them." Mago's hand went for his Bag of Tricks. He undid the flap. "I have a notion that our guests might appreciate a little magic." He brought out what appeared to be a small bundle of tapers.

"Lead me forward a few steps, Cerdic. They won't kill us until they discover who we are and why we are here. But do not panic!"

They waited. There was no movement from the Hsiung-nu.

"What're they 'angin' on for?" groaned Silenos. "Y'd think they'd never set eyes on t'likes of us 'afore."

With an escort of two riders, the leader of the warriors came slowly down the hill. He made a sign. His escort dismounted. They tipped the tents from the horses and the yak. They slit the ropes binding the tents and kicked them open. Puzzled, they stared across the brilliant sand at the travellers. So little, here in the desert; not enough to exist on, and nothing to barter with?

The leader rode up to Mago. He did not hurry to speak. His piercing eyes rested on the members of the caravan one by one, then reverted to Mago.

The wind drew back the mask from his face, revealing a sallow skin and short-cropped beard. His flesh was a mass of scars. His thin lips hardly seemed to move as he spoke, in a language none in the caravan had heard before.

Mago attempted to reply in gestures. He measured the distance they had come, over mountain and river, from the West. He tried to explain the disaster that had befallen the caravan, but the horseman merely pointed his finger at Mago's staff, then at the swords worn by Festus and Thyrsis. They pitched them into the sand.

He was sufficiently interested in Festus' Roman broad-sword to dismount and pick it up. He turned it over on his hand as though such a weapon were familiar to him. Thrusting it through his belt, he remounted and, without another look, rode back to his former position along the shadowy curve of the dunes. The other riders joined him.

There was no sound but that of the wind. The leader of the horsemen glanced along his ranks, silhouetted against the light.

"They're going to kill us," said Thyrsis. "He's raising his arm!"

The spears of the Hsiung-nu were held high in the air.

"Wait!" roared Mago, advancing three strides. "Wait!" His voice rose hauntingly in the dry hollow of sand. After stretching himself to his full height, he dropped to his knees, bringing his elbows and arms close in to his chest. The next moment, he held out his right hand. Clutched between his fingers was a burning stick, a flame that darted and fizzed.

He stood. He waved the burning stick in an arc above his head. He walked forward and made as if to present the flame to the leader of the Hsiung-nu. His gesture caused a stir of movement among the previously still ranks. Heads turned, horses stepped back, spears wavered.

Mago doused the flame between his fingers. Hesitantly, and perhaps against his better judgment, the warrior approached Mago. His eyes were fixed warily upon him. He was driven on by curiosity. He suddenly grabbed the stick.

He held it close to him as Mago had done. He thrust it out as Mago had done. He waved it, but no flame appeared.

The instant the warrior's attention rested on the spent stick, Mago brought fire into the world once more. To the Hsiung-nu, the second stick seemed to derive its flame from Mago's fingers. "For you," said Mago.

Bravely, for his men were watching, the warrior took the flaming stick into his own hand. There was no change in his expression. His gaze left Mago's face for scarcely a moment. Then he hurled the stick away. He wheeled his horse round. He galloped back to the safety of his men.

He was afraid—and he would kill this magician before he could use his powers to harm the warriors of the Hsiung-nu. He barked an order for the spears to be raised again.

Mago half-turned to his friends. "Alas, there are no more tricks. I have brought death upon us."

"Then we'll die fighting," shouted Thyrsis, wrenching a large stone out of the sand.

"Wait!" Mago warned. "What's that I can hear?"

More horsemen were surging in from the east, yelling greetings. They circled the top of the dunes, as if celebrating a recent victory. There was a confused mingling of horses and riders, then the ranks opened. All arms went up in salute as the new leader passed through.

"Is he clad in scarlet, like a flame, Cerdic?" asked Mago.

Cerdic was astonished at what he saw. His words stumbled out: "No, not scarlet, Uncle . . . Not at all! But it's . . . It's a—"

"Well swallow me ladle!" exclaimed Silenos. "Is this another o' them merryages you talked of, Master? That general o'theirs is nothin' but a—lass!"

9

Daughter of the Fire King

In every detail she was dressed like the Hsiung-nu—black
hood to keep off the sun's rays, tunic of animal skins, black fur
boots reaching up to her knees. But round her neck was a Seric
scarf, white as fresh-fallen snow, with a brilliant sheen. She
carried a longbow and a sheaf of arrows on her back; and like
the other Hsiung-nu, she rode her Farghana horse—a handsome piebald—without saddle.

"If she's a day over fifteen," estimated Silenos, "I'll eat my
weight in sand! And she's a beauty!"

Cerdic described the girls' scarf to his uncle. "Do you hear
that, Widuhar?" Mago called softly. "She wears about her
throat the same miraculous cloth which your Parthian enemies
made into golden banners."

"Aye, Master," replied Widuhar. "We'll soon have their
secret . . . But not a word to the Empress that I am Lord of
Persepolis. Speak of me as just a humble cowherd."

The girl had been listening to the leader of her horsemen. At
the same time she gazed at the caravan. He was asking her,
should the execution be carried out? Not at once, seemed to be
her decision.

She was coming down.

A few paces in front of Mago, she stopped. Immediately
Cerdic noticed beads of blood seeping from the neck of her

Farghana horse. Slung on a leather thong across her shoulder was a jewel-handled sword. It was smeared with blood of another kind. Cerdic also noticed a wound on the girl's forearm. This had been bound hastily with a torn cloth which had not entirely staunched the bleeding.

Once again, each member of the caravan was scrutinised, but this time by eyes full of intelligence and beauty as well as ferocity. At first, she spoke in her own language, pointing at Mago who replied, "We are merchants, my lady, travelling from the West. Our carriers and our guide deserted us in the night."

The girl amazed them by answering in their own language. "They fly now with the Raven of Death." She turned and signalled to her men. One led the lost camels and yaks to the top of the dunes.

She rode closer to Mago, as though to test his sightlessness. "Speak no lies, Blind One, to Xandria, Princess of the Hsiung-nu . . . Torcis says you are a magician, sent by our enemies."

"Gracious Princess, we come as friends, from Carthage, from Rome—"

"Rome! That cannot be. You lie!"

All spears were raised.

"It's true, Princess," burst in Cerdic. "Please believe us!" As he spoke, his arm brushed the strings of his harp. The sound attracted the Princess. She stared at the harp. Cerdic held it in playing position. He strummed a gentle cord—then offered the harp to the Princess.

He knew she would have liked to take it. She was fascinated by it, suddenly child-like with wonder. But she became stern again. "None, Blind One, has ever crossed the Roof of the World." She paused. "None but the Square Arms."

"Square Arms?" Festus stepped forward. "You know of them?—they are who we seek! My father—."

"Silence! The Square Arms serve only the Hsiung-nu. Speak not of them!" She rounded on Mago. "Is this why you have come, Blind One, to work evil magic on my father's glory, when he prepares to destroy the peoples of the Emperor of Heaven for ever?"

"We are merchants, Princess, wishing only to trade the purple cloth of our country . . ."

Before Mago could finish, the Princess gave orders. The camels and yaks were driven down, their loads scattered on the ground. A roll of purple cloth was handed to her, and her anger faded.

In a less harsh voice, she said, "It has been predicted, in the burnt shell of the turtle, that an Eyeless Stranger will come among the Hsiung-nu . . . Torcis calls for your death, but that will be for my father to decide." There was something else. "If you are only a merchant, Blind One, how can you make fire grow from your fingers?"

Mago drew another "Firestick" from his pocket, keeping a small pebble hidden in the palm of his hand. He struck the stick against the pebble.

The Princess was startled and her horse almost bucked.

"Pray do not be afraid, Princess," reassured Mago. "This gift of magic fire I bring to your father." He snapped out the flame. "We come in friendship, and with other gifts—necklaces, brooches, by the finest craftsmen in Carthage."

The Princess shook her head. Her eyes were on Cerdic's harp, with its beautifully inlaid dragon, breathing sparks of fire. He offered it to her. She would have taken it but for a warning voice from Torcis. "You are our prisoners!" she asserted. She reined her piebald mare. "Death alone is the gift of those who disobey: you will follow the Hsiung-nu." She shouted a command. In response, the Hsiung-nu let go a spine-chilling howl.

"March away!"

"Under royal protection," stated Mago in his Log, "we have survived five days of travel which have been among the hardest of our whole journey. The Hsiung-nu ride like the wind. They take no rest till nightfall, and by first light they are ready to gallop for another day.

"But for the Princess's kindness, Torcis, the leader of the horsemen, would have left us to die in the sand. Because of her, we rest; we are fed as well as her warriors and I am permitted to dictate my Log to Cerdic in peace.

"We have witnessed much evidence of the brutal and quar-relsome nature of the Hsiung-nu. At the least provocation they fight among themselves and invariably one of the combatants is left dying in the desert sand. Even a blind man has no difficulty recognising the approach of a Hsiung-nu, for they smell abom-inably, believing that water will rub off their skins and leave them naked to the bone.

"Women, it seems, are permitted the saving grace of an occasional salt bath—or at least princesses are! My tablets of soap have been the gift Princess Xandria has allowed herself to accept, though we had to control many a smile in teaching her that it could not be used without water.

"She desires to be friendly towards us and is eager to learn of life in the West, but we are not the first Romans she has met. Festus is convinced—and I am inclined to believe he is right—that the Square Arms she mentions, yet will not speak of in detail, are the Roman soldiers in whose tracks we have followed for so many months. We endeavour to convince her that our intention is not to persuade the Square Arms to return to the West. Always, when we are close to allaying her fears, Torcis appears in her shadow, for ever reminding her that we might be the enemies of her father, the Fire king.

"Most of all, the Princess admires Cerdic's skill upon the harp. The children of the Emperor of Heaven have such things, she says, but not the Hsiung-nu; the cries of battle are their only music. She would have Cerdic teach her to play, but seems afraid of what her warriors would say of one who, even for a moment, laid down sword and spear for a weapon of peace.

"Indeed Xandria is like no woman we have ever encountered. The day of our meeting, she had led her warriors against a troop of Seric bowmen, killing every one of them and decapitating them so that their souls would not be admitted into the Kingdom of Darkness. She boasts of the number of the enemy she has slain.

"It is my belief that the Princess's overwhelming wish is to prove to her father that she is in every respect as brave and daring as a son. Cerdic has been challenged to a horse race, Festus to a contest in throwing the javelin, when we arrive at the King's summer camp.

"She speaks reverently of her brother, the King's only surviving son, who is held captive, it seems, by the Emperor of Heaven. To be robbed thus of a son has filled the Fire King with undying hatred for his enemy.

"Alas, we have arrived here in inauspicious days, for the great war between the Hsiung-nu and the people of the Emperor of Heaven, threatened for so long, is about to take place. The Fire King will, we are told, be in a celebrating mood. He has just returned from a successful attack upon the country of the Sogdians. They became guilty of the greatest of all crimes in his eyes—friendship with the Emperor of Heaven.

"Finally, before our arrival at the camp—and who knows, before our execution—I commit to my Log the curious name of the King, which none of us can properly pronounce. It is JZH-JZH! Xandria pronounces it Juzz-Juzz; yet whichever way it falls upon the ear, it strikes terror in the hearts of those who have suffered at his hands, or heard of his reputation.

"The Hsiung-nu proudly boast of the King's other name— the Merciless One."

Cerdic stored his own memories of the past days. He remembered how the desert ahead had turned white like a vast sunlit lake. His surprise had caused Xandria to smile for the very first time. "You wish to swim?"

Begrimed with sand and sweat, Cerdic had responded eagerly. He rode his hardest to keep up with the Princess. She was no longer just smiling, she was laughing. Her hair streamed in the wind. Her sword-hilt glinted in the sun.

They had reached within a quarter of a mile of the lake when the cause of the Princess's laughter became clear to Cerdic. He reined Pythias sharply. The white sheen on the surface of the lake was not caused by sunlight at all.

"It's salt! A sea of salt!" He rode nearer. "There's enough to fill Silenos' stews for a million years." He glanced at Xandria. He smiled. Then he began to laugh.

They dismounted together. Xandria waited till Cerdic had gathered a pocketful of salt. "What is your name?" she asked.

"Cerdic."

"You shall be my friend, Cerdic, for when the Princess likes a person, she keeps no secret of it. When we gallop towards the ranks of the Emperor of Heaven, you may ride beside me."

Cerdic concealed his alarm. He swallowed hard. She was expecting a reply from him. "I shall cherish your friendship,

Princess." He paused. "In fact you're a much better princess than any I've read about in stories."

Xandria nodded. She seemed glad to know she was better than storybook princesses. "Now we shall have that race, I think."

Beyond the lake of salt, the glitter of sun on water was no longer an illusion. Flocks of yellow plumaged flamingoes strutted above their reflections. Shell-duck wheeled in the clear blue air and Cerdic was able to identify for his uncle many other birds, such as grebe, willow warblers and redstarts.

Cerdic described the changing landscape to his uncle: "It's getting more and more fantastic. There are great sandbanks ahead, thirty or forty feet high, with sheer sides. Like war ships in a convoy."

"War ships is right," said Festus. "Look, on the prow of every one of them is a Hsiung-nu guard. From up there they could spot an advancing army twenty miles away."

As they passed between the desert ships, Cerdic noticed several dark specks circling in the sky. They grew larger, hovering on huge black wings. "They're bigger than crows," he said, describing them to Mago. "Evil-looking things," Many of them were congregating on the ground, bald-pated, wing-beating, jostling, lunging downwards with long, curved beaks.

Silenos yelped in disgust. "'Orrible! 'Orrible! Them's 'uman bodies they're peckin' at!"

Scores of bodies were scattered beside the track, some so rotted by time and the sharp appetite of the vultures that their skeletons protruded from the despoiled flesh. They were wreathed in swarms of flies.

"Their heads are severed," observed Festus, choking on his words.

The stench of the corpses spread like the vapour from an open sewer, and the members of the caravan pressed hands, sleeves, caps, to their faces to prevent themselves retching.

Mago had one comment to make, "Is it any wonder that the Emperor of Heaven constructed a wall, as I have heard tell, longer and higher than the world has ever seen, to keep out such a monstrous people?"

There were to be even more disturbing sights. The ships of sand, more and more heavily guarded by the Hsiung-nu, were moored closer together. Eventually, they resembled a harbour at the centre of which was the camp of the Hsiung-nu, protected on all sides by high rocks.

The entrance to the camp was lined with wooden spikes, each surmounted by the blood-dripping head of a Seric prisoner.

Princess Xandria came galloping back to the members of the caravan, a look of triumph on her face. "Do you see—my father's enemies! So end all those who defy the Fire King!"

She seemed to want the captives to demonstrate their admiration of the scene before them. Their silence stung her to anger. "Why do you not speak? Blind One, has your boy not described to you the trophies of my father's greatness?"

Mago nodded.

"Then what have you to say?" The Princess's voice split with anger when Mago still withheld his praise. "Speak, Blind One, or feel the sharp tongue of my whip!"

"I can only conclude, Princess," answered Mago slowly, "that the Roman warriors whose shadows have retreated eastwards before us, are not to be found in your father's camp." He hesitated, but only for a moment. "Such ravages of the fallen no Roman would tolerate."

The caravan had witnessed Princess Xandria's spiritedness and her generosity. Now they shrank from the flash of her temper.

"That is where you speak lies into the air, Blind One! You will soon discover that the Square Arms fight only for the Fire King and obey his every command..." She broke off suddenly. Her handsome eyes narrowed. She glanced at Cerdic as though unwilling to include him in her condemnation. But her warriors were looking on.

"You trick me!" A little of the fire had gone from her expression. She was less confident than before, uncertain. Aware of this, she was determined to assert herself.

"By your weak words, Blind One, you have displeased me. I shall not speak for you to my father, as I had intended. His will be final!"

She spun round and raced between the fly-smothered heads. The Hsiung-nu snarled their own displeasure. They whipped the caravan along, almost forcing their prisoners on to the spikes.

Once a grassy knoll irrigated by a stream that issued from a plateau of rock, the camp had been transformed into sunbaked mud. It was littered from end to end with the debris of feasting, fighting and execution. The ground was dotted black with extinguished bonfires. It was covered with the leftovers of a thousand meals—offal, bones, the skulls of sheep and cattle; and with unwanted booty—clothes, sandals, broken spears, bundles of human hair. There were also curious piles everywhere, of bevelled wooden implements which Festus thought looked like crossbows.

Save for a few warriors squatting round a campfire and

sharing a drink which filled them with loud merriment, the camp was deserted. Then Cerdic observed a gap in the far rocks. Xandria, now dismounted, was leading them towards it.

She halted. She signalled for silence and immediately a chorus of droning voices was to be heard, a hundred warriors repeating the cry of a single voice. Smoke fanned up in grey-blue clouds, permitting momentary glimpses of a figure at an altar built into the rock.

A figure dressed from head to foot in scarlet. "The Fire King!" whispered Cerdic to his uncle.

The drone had become a discordant wail. It soared to a crescendo. The scarlet figure turned. He seemed to be part of the flames, unreal, floating on the waves of heat from the fire. He had sacrificed a bullock on the altar. He held up the bleeding knife. He gave a short, high-pitched scream. His warriors answered him, plunging their spears into the air.

Beside the scarlet figure was another, his face painted with crude bars of colour, wearing a feathered head-dress and a tunic that appeared to be made up entirely of bones. At his belt hung white skulls. A closer look would have shown that the boots he wore were of human ears sewn together.

"Nazir, my father's wizard," the Princess announced proudly. "With the magic of Nazir, the Fire King's enemies fall as grass before the scythe!"

Nazir advanced on the flames. They sparked and danced, and the assembly roared as the tips of the flames turned green.

The ceremony continued until the sun, having touched the pinnacle of rocks and flooded them with its own fire, slipped from view. The chanting ceased. Nazir was gone and the flames died down as though in obedience to their master. The clearing before the altar could be seen in every detail.

Against the rock was pitched a very large, square-topped

tent, made of a material which caused Widuhar to gasp, for once again, here was the shiny brilliance of the Parthian banners, of Xandria's white scarf. It was dyed scarlet, and its surface rippled in the breeze like the sunset across water.

The Princess returned from her father's tent. "You will wait! And on your knees, with your faces to the ground."

The members of the caravan did as they were commanded, hemmed in by the inquisitive Hsiung-nu who allowed them scarcely enough room to breathe.

Silenos in particular attracted the attention of some of the warriors. His fatness amused them. They prodded him, made jokes, and roared with laughter. "Pray Jupiter they don't mean to 'ave me fer supper!" He was forced on to his feet, urged to dance. A spear lodged between his legs and he fell heavily, causing the Hsiung-nu to leap about in mirth.

All at once, the laughter died away. The warriors opened their ranks. They dipped their spears in greeting as Jzh-Jzh, the Fire King, the Merciless One, approached. He wore, not Sericum as Cerdic had thought, but scarlet leather.

He held out in front of him a freshly severed head and the Hsiung-nu cheered at the sight of it.

The head had so occupied Cerdic's gaze that he did not at first notice how the King's face was totally concealed by a veil of thinnest Sericum. Cerdic gave a shudder, for it was like setting eyes upon a man without a face. He could not stop himself looking from his lowly position on the ground. The veil glistened in the fading light. The breeze touched it, brushed it inwards—and Cerdic suddenly knew: the King had no nose.

There was complete silence as Jzh-Jzh spoke, in the language of the Romans and in a voice as strange as his appearance, a voice of one whose vocal chords had been damaged, and could only utter deep-throated, breathless sounds.

"Stand up, the Blind One, who brings magic from the West." Mago got slowly to his feet, continuing to bow low. "You have come, stranger, to rob me of my warriors of the Square Arms."

"No!" replied Mago.

"Be silent!" Spearpoints bristled around Mago's body. "You will speak only when the Fire King orders you to speak." He held up the severed head. "Soon, by dawn, I will cure you of your blindness, stranger. For I know you!" His broken voice rose to a shriek. "I have expected you—the Blind Stranger, as in the prophecy: None shall defeat Jzh-Jzh save a two-headed dragon, heralded by a Blind One from across the Great Desert."

Jzh-Jzh hurled the head down into the sand. Then he stepped forward and spat into Mago's face. "Thus do I scorn the prophecies!" He beckoned to his wizard, Nazir, who stepped from the lengthening shadows. The bones of his weird costume clacked together as he moved. "By the magic of Nazir," the Fire King declared, "the prophecy shall be defeated. Jzh-Jzh shall float in majesty upon the blood of his enemies—and none shall be spared, not a child new-born nor a woman enfeebled with age. Nor will a single house of the Emperor of Heaven's people be left standing, nor a field of wheat unburnt. The only rivers will be rivers of blood, the hills will be mountains of their dead. But most of all, I will rob the world of their memory. If they seek to bury their precious books, the Hsiung-nu will discover every one and make a fire of them that will be seen as far away as Rome. If the wind steals their womanly songs, and the music they so love, I will destroy the wind itself.

"Thus will Jzh-Jzh avenge his lost son!"

There was silence. The King's words seemed to ricochet

through the rocks. Then the Hsiung-nu, who understood only the anger of his speech, screamed and cavorted in the air, shaking their spears. They pressed forward, confident that Jzh-Jzh had given the order for the execution of these strangers. But he held up his hand. They waited.

"Before you die, Blind one, you will show me the secret of the fire that grows through your fingers . . . You hesitate. Has the magic gone from you that my daughter speaks of? Ha! As I thought, the power of Nazir has put your spirits to flight." He repeated this, in his own language, and Nazir's painted face nodded in confirmation. Yet when he turned back to Mago, he saw the flame spurt from the explorer's fingers and on to a stick which he held in front of his face.

The Hsiung-nu shrank back a pace, their eyes on the Firestick, then on their King.

Mago blew out the Firestick as Jzh-Jzh snatched it from him. The King held it cautiously. He touched the end with his fingers. He waved it in the air.

Mago ventured to speak: "O mighty king, your wizard Nazir will surely be able to breathe fire into the stick."

Jzh-Jzh was impressed. He frowned at Torcis, his general, who made to spear Mago down for his presumption in speaking. "Let it be so!" He signalled to Nazir. The hopes of the caravan quickened. "We'll win, we'll win!" thought Cerdic, keeping his fingers crossed.

But Nazir was not to be tricked. He did not step forward. He did not allow himself even a look at the Firestick. He spoke, at the same time shaking his head solemnly.

The King seemed well pleased. "Nazir refuses the Blind One's challenge—for that which has been touched by your magic remains under a spell for five days and five nights."

Torcis was impatient to put an end to the strangers. He

pointed towards the great cooking fires where sheep were being roasted on spits. Supper was ready. The Hsiung-nu were hungry from a long day's riding.

At that moment, a slave-boy passed, carrying a bowl of fruit and a tall clay drinking vessel to Princess Xandria's tent. "Bring me those, boy!" growled the Fire King. He tossed away the fruit and swallowed the contents of the drinking vessel.

"Make magic with those, Blind One." He dropped bowl and cup in front of Mago. "Turn them into fire—and I spare your lives one hour!"

Mago reached forward. He was about to touch them when Jzh-Jzh ordered his hands away. "Describe them to me, Cerdic," sighed the blind explorer, trying to hide his despondence.

"A bronze bowl, shallow, with a curved lip round it . . ."

"How wide?"

"About a hand-span . . . And the goblet—that's got straight sides, nine or ten inches high. Nothing else."

"Well?" insisted the King. "Where is your magic?"

Mago hesitated. He was wrapped in thought. He tugged at his beard. Then he raised his sightless eyes. He answered confidently. "With those objects, O Fire King, I challenge your wizard once more . . . Not to make fire, but to demonstrate the simplest of magic."

Xandria had come forward into the torchlit circle. "For my sake, father, allow him this favour."

All Mago asked for in addition to the bowl and the goblet was an oil-lamp and a little water, which one of the Hsiung-nu brought from Xandria's tent.

The quiet was intense. "I would ask the Princess has she a ring on her finger? Yes? Then would she most kindly place it in the dish, near the rim? Now, cover the ring with water."

This was done. "I call upon Nazir the Wizard to remove the ring with his bare fingers, yet not touch a single drop of water. He can make use of the goblet and the lighted lamp if all other magic fails him."

The King warmed to this challenge almost with boyish delight. Behind the mask of Sericum, his mutilated face could be seen to be smiling. He called to his wizard. "Nazir will make the water vanish—and he shall have the Blind One's head as a prize!"

10

Message of alarm

The light from the bonfires sent flickering shadows across the camp of the Hsiung-nu. This was the time of feasting, then of games of battle and wild drinking of rice wine. But all was delayed for Nazir, the mighty wizard, to complete his long ritual dance and his howling incantations.

Yet neither dancing nor incantation removed the water from the shallow dish. The ring remained sparkling under the surface. King Jzh-Jzh's faith in his wizard changed to disgust. He advanced on Mago. "Nazir will roast on a sheep-spit if you succeed, Blind One. If you fail, you both roast together!"

Calmly Mago said: "In order that I shall not be accused of passing magic through my fingers, let the Princess do as I instruct her." The King gave his consent.

"Now Princess, please place the lighted lamp in the centre of the bowl." She did so. "Take the goblet and turn it upside down. Very carefully lower it over the lamp . . . Gently!"

"It is done," replied the Princess.

"I see no magic!" rapped the King impatiently.

"Watch the water, if you please, O Fire King."

As Mago spoke, the water began to drain away, leaving the ring at the side of the bowl exposed for Xandria to retrieve, dry-fingered.

The fact that Mago's success had been so simply achieved

filled the Fire King with added rage towards his wizard. He ordered him to be seized. "To the fire!" he roared. "Make roasted meat of him!"

Yet Mago's raised voice came at the King through the confusion of voices. "Wait, O Fire King . . . My own magic will die if one should lose his life because of it." He made Jzh-Jzh pause. "And I confess that it is not magic at all—but something greater."

Intrigued, Jzh-Jzh allowed his wizard to be released, and Nazir was left to shrink away into the shadows. "Greater than magic, you say, Blind One?"

"Science, O Fire King."

"Science? I know of no such word."

"Nazir could as easily have removed the ring as I, if he had known how . . . The flame under the goblet drank up a portion of the air and thus the water was sucked upwards. See, lift the goblet and the water will return to the dish."

Tentatively, Jzh-Jzh raised the goblet.

"You will observe that the flame is extinguished, for in a confined space fire consumes that portion of the air which feeds it. Then the flame dies."

At first moved by admiration, Jzh-Jzh suddenly became cold again. "It is clear that your journey across the Roof of the World was neither to bring gifts of magic to the Fire King nor to seek out the Square Arms. Such a journey, for one of your kind, could have but one destination—the people of the Emperor of Heaven. They would respect your science. They would have a place for you . . . But not I!"

Xandria was pulling at her father's sleeve. The Princess knew—they all knew—that only she could delay their summary execution. She whispered in her father's ear, and what she said met with his approval. He gave orders to Torcis, who hastened away to return carrying a pile of wooden implements—the same that Festus had guessed were the components of crossbows. He cast the pile down in front of Mago.

"My daughter has reminded me, O Blind One, that Jzh-Jzh has need of science—in one respect. You and your followers will be spared, if, by dawn, you have assembled that crossbow from the pieces that lie before you."

The King's voice conveyed pride and regret. "But for those crossbows which the warriors of the Emperor of Heaven wield with such deadly skill, my people would have driven their nation to the bottom of their wide rivers. Like bolts of fire their arrows come at us and time without number we have been driven back from their Wall of Giants."

He stooped for the pieces of the crossbow, then hurled them down again. "Yet not once have we been able to use their captured bows. Not once! In the very throes of death the soldiers touch their weapons in a secret place—and they fall into pieces which not even Nazir can put together again. We kill them by the thousand, but not one complete bow do they allow to fall into our hands.

"Discover their secret for us, Blind One, and you shall not only have your life. You shall take back to your people a prize that will make you wealthy beyond measure. The little worms from whose backs the Seres spin their miraculous cloth are as closely-guarded as the Emperor of Heaven himself. Succeed, and you shall have them. Fail, and the vultures will partake of both you and your science!"

Too hungry, too thirsty and too anxious to sleep, Cerdic lay watching his uncle attempting to assemble the pieces of the crossbow for the twentieth time. "In this matter," he had sighed, "my heart fights my hands. If I put the bow together I

129

save our lives and sacrifice perhaps hundreds of others."

"But it's only one bow," Cerdic had argued.

Mago shook his head. "Many bows—one secret." Yet he had persisted. He was curious, and when he had suffered one setback after another, he warmed to the challenge. "Whoever designed this piece of engineering," he confessed, "was a genius."

The noise of riotous feasting carried across the night camp. Sated with mutton, drunk with rice wine, the Hsiung-nu had begun what, to them, were games, but to strangers unaccustomed to such expressions of violence, were terrifying spectacles.

The game that aroused most merriment involved two combatants armed with javelins but no shields. They stood in circles drawn in the sand about thirty yards apart. There appeared to be only one rule, that neither warrior was allowed out of his circle until the other lay helplessly wounded. The victors earned stoups of rice wine, while the vanquished were dragged uncaringly into the shadows.

Festus wondered, "Could my father be an ally of such horrible barbarians?"

For the twenty-first time the crossbow dropped to pieces in Mago's hand.

"Don't be botherin' yer'ead wi'it, Master," recommended Silenos. "We'll be t' vultoors' breakfast in t'mornin', whatever 'appens. So you get some rest."

Mago did not hear him. He was closed against his surroundings. He felt no hunger, and was as absorbed in his task as he might be with a mathematical problem.

He thought aloud. "It's clear that the pull of the bowstring is reduced by a triple compound lever, whose parts are constructed in such a way that only the trigger can release the string, yet the pull of the string holds the pieces of the bow firmly in place."

"You were right 'bout them folks beyond t'North Wind bein' clever, Master," mused Silenos.

"A pity," came in Thyrsis, "that their cleverness threatens to be the death of us."

Still ignoring the voices around him, Mago began to describe again the items before him: "Three movable pieces. Two crosswise pins which are inserted on each side of the case. Here is the upper vertical arm with the prongs for the string, here the horizontal section resting inside the case . . ."

Cerdic's exhaustion was slowly overcoming his determination to stay awake. His uncle's words were lulling him to sleep. They were like lights on moving water, shining, then gone. ". . . which in turn is pivoted . . . fits into a notch in the third piece . . . pivoted upon the first pin . . . remove the pins from the stick and . . ."

He was adrift, a light on the water, dreaming of vultures and severed heads, of the shrunken skulls on Nazir's belt, of the Fire King's noseless face behind the mask of glistening Sericum. And he dreamed of Xandria slipping from the shadows and kneeling beside him, nudging his arm.

But was it a dream? He stirred. He felt the hand against his arm again.

"Cerdic, wake up!" She was gazing down at him. Her finger was at her lips. "You must hurry. The sleep of the sun is almost over."

"Hurry?" he looked around him. Festus was alert, ready to spring up. Farther off, having sought seclusion to concentrate on his task, was Mago, his back to the rest.

"I have horses waiting," instructed the Princess. "While my

father's guards hang their heads in drunken sleep, I will show you a path that will lead you from the camp unseen."

Cerdic nodded. He was on his feet. "I'll tell Uncle."

"No!" The Princess blocked his way. "The Blind One must remain here. If he teaches the crossbow to fire again, his life will be spared. For you, there will be no mercy. Hurry, now!"

Cerdic did not move. He stared at Xandria in amazement. "Escape without my Uncle? Without even saying a word to him?" He turned to Festus and the others who were awake and ready to flee. "The Princess offers you freedom. May the gods go with you!"

Decisively, he lowered himself to the ground. He looked up at the Princess. She did not understand. It was as though she had been slapped in the face.

Festus had also returned to where he had been lying. "For a moment, I forgot myself. It is not possible, Princess."

Unbelievingly, Xandria watched Tryphon and Widuhar, Silenos and finally Thyrsis squat down again in their former positions. Her eyes suddenly filled with tears. "For an old man, who has lived his full years, you will surrender all that lies before you? They have taught you bad things in the West!" She spun round, ashamed of revealing her womanly heart, and ran for her tent.

At almost the same instant, Mago, unaware of the drama that had gone on behind him, gave a murmur of deep satisfaction. "Now that was a puzzle which nearly had the beating of me!" He held up the crossbow for the others to see. "In one piece, my friends, and ready to fire a bolt straight and true!"

As if to celebrate Mago's triumph, a pale jewel of light rolled across the eastward plain. No less promptly, King Jzh-Jzh strode from among his drunkenly sleeping warriors.

His progress was halted by a sharp, commanding call from

Mago. "Before you step closer, O Fire King, let your oath be renewed, that my life and those of my companions be spared ... Or I will cast this weapon once more in pieces at your feet! The secret of the crossbow will die with me."

The King assented. "So long as you labour to provide the Hsiung-nu with weapons to devastate the armies of the Emperor of Heaven, the Blind one's companions shall live."

Attention was diverted to shouts coming from the far end of the camp. A spear beat against metal. The Hsiung-nu darted up from sleep. Through the rows of severed heads, through the ranks of warriors, past the declining fires, galloped a horseman. His black tunic was covered with the dust of travel and his Farghana horse steamed with sweat.

The rider looked to neither right nor left, plunging directly on towards the scarlet-clad King. He reined in in a cloud of sand. His shrill message needed no questioning, for the King immediately yelled orders which set the whole camp in feverish motion.

Jzh-Jzh raced for his horse as it was brought to him. He was up. He glanced back over his shoulder at Mago. "We shall have need of your services, Blind One ... The Emperor of Heaven marches on my capital!"

For a brief while, Cerdic forgot the dark fateful days which seemed to lie ahead. There was sunlight, birdsong and a warm breeze from the south. Pytheus trotted powerfully beneath him, his hooves no longer impeded by soft sand or tracks of dried mud. They pounded along grassy slopes, echoed through bare green valleys, whispered over the needle-carpets of pine-woods.

Xandria and Cerdic were friends again. "We bear grudges

only against the Emperor of Heaven," she declared. Suspicious of what Torcis, her father's general, might do with the prisoners if he were left alone with them, the Princess rode with the caravan.

"You seem to be glad there's going to be a war," Cerdic told her.

"Oh yes!" The Princess gave a radiant, bewitching smile. "If my people have no enemy to fight, they fight among themselves—and that I do not like."

They came to a wide, shallow river which the Princess called the Talass. "Two more hours' riding to the north and we shall reach my father's capital. You must not expect anything grand such as Carthage or Rome, for the Hsiung-nu are a wandering people. Walls and roofs, we detest—not like the Square Arms who persuaded my father that only walls can save us from the wrath of the Emperor of Heaven."

"Is it not possible, Princess," Mago asked, "for the Hsiung-nu to live at peace with the Seric people?"

Xandria tossed her black hair proudly. "The Hsiung-nu can as easily live without war as the flower without sun and rain. We cannot change!"

They rode on until afternoon faded into evening. The weary miles had begun to tell on Mago. Physically exhausted, he had also succumbed to a profound sadness. To Cerdic, he confessed, "The tide of events has turned against us, my boy. How many hundreds of miles have we traversed, how many times have we risked our lives and the lives of others in search of a civilisation whose magnificence matches that of Greece herself, only to find ourselves among the ranks of her mortal enemies?"

Silenos alone remained of good cheer. His voice was the first to break a long silence. "Well tickle me feet wi'a goose feather! Look yonder!"

Away to the east, where the Talass curved in a broad loop, was the capital city of the Fire King. Silenos was laughing. "It's nothin' but a pimple o' a town, Master!"

"But it's well defended," observed Festus. His interest quickened. "Those are Roman palisades—surely!" He glanced joyfully at Tryphon.

Xandria, who alone could have answered the burning questions Festus wished to ask, had ridden on, leaving the surly and uncommunicative Torcis in command of the caravan.

Cerdic described the scene to his uncle. "We're still half a mile off. I can see two wooden walls. The outer one's made of tall logs with sharp points. Fifteen feet high, I'd say. The inner wall's thicker and higher, with watchtowers and slits to fire through. That must be twenty-five feet at least. There's a main gate with the biggest of the towers on either side."

"Them Seric folks is goin' t'get their toes wet," added Silenos. "Can y' see t'moat? An' farther in, there's some nasty-lookin' 'oles in t'ground."

"No drunken spearmen had the wit to build all this, Master," said Thyrsis. "Only skilled carpenters could've crenellated that inner wall— and Roman carpenters at that. Who doubts now that the Merciless One's fortunes hang by a Roman thread?"

Festus would have raced on, but Mago urged patience. "There is hope, but let caution rule you for the present."

Cerdic knew the doubts that would be plaguing his friend's mind at this moment. His own mouth was dry with expectation. His pulses beat like drums. "Show me your father's ring again, Festus."

With a nervous smile, the young Roman displayed the onyx ring bearing the image of the piper and the dancing dog. "I know, Cerdic! In my heart I know we shall find my father."

"Should we do so," said Mago, "then our journey will not have been in vain."

King Jzh-Jzh and his warriors were not far ahead now. Though he had galloped hard on hearing the news of the advance of the Emperor of Heaven, the Merciless One had chosen to approach his capital at a pace fitting a monarch whose custom was to cause panic in others, not show it himself.

Indeed his intention appeared to be to delay entry into the city for as long as possible. Still a quarter of a mile from the water-filled moat, he had ordered his men into two battlelines, facing each other across a hundred paces.

Then Jzh-Jzh began to drill them. The spectacle that followed would have been sufficient to convince even the bitterest enemy of the Hsiung-nu that here were the finest horsemen in the world.

On foot, in camp, they were a rabble. On horseback they were disciplined, as swift in response to commands as the Farghana horses were to understand what their riders required of them. Between warrior and horse there was an uncanny "oneness" of mind, gained by endless practice and the result of generations of partnership between horse and man.

The battlelines thundered forwards head on. Horse passed horse without touching. The lines wheeled. They charged again, altering direction at the last moment. Without slackening speed, the horsemen dismounted, ran several breath-taking paces then flipped back into riding position. They plunged across each other's path, making a cross-stitch pattern.

To gasps of admiration from the onlookers, the Hsiung-nu now raced two abreast. Spears in hand, they leapt each other's horses. As they sprang back to their own mounts they exchanged spears.

"We'd mek a fortune i'Cathage wi't'likes o' these," nodded Silenos.

"Clearly there's someone in the city the Fire King wishes to impress," said Mago as Cerdic described the Hsiung-nu display.

"Who else but the Host of a Thousand?" cried Widuhar. "I've had a vision of them in all their glory, beyond the walls . . . Believe my words, friendly shepherds—the Prince of Persepolis has spoken! And in my vision I can hear the very thoughts of their general: there will be one last battle, a mighty battle."

"And then?" asked Festus, anxious, willing himself to believe.

"Then?" Widuhar stared up into the starlit evening. "All I see is a flag."

"There he goes again," grumbled Thyrsis, "on about his precious Golden Banners."

"No! Strangely, I no longer see the Golden Banners, but a white flag with an emblem shrouded in mist."

The Hsiung-nu had re-formed into two columns for their final sortie. They roared across the plain, dark shadows over the lightless ground. Then, as though he had popped up from the earth like a rabbit, a warrior emerged carrying a lighted torch.

The riders enveloped him; and in seconds they all bore torches. Young flames spluttered, grew, and danced on the black masks of the Hsiung-nu.

Slowly they advanced over the moat towards the towered gates of the city. They stretched out until there were several yards between each horseman. They became an avenue of torches, straight and wide, from the gates to the position of the Fire King some five hundred yards away.

Jzh-Jzh remained still, facing the gates.

From the inner palisade of the city a roll of drums reverberated through the silence. The gates swung open. The entrance glowed with torchlight. There was a brief emptiness, a waiting.

Into the circle of light and shadow came figures, under the arched gate and out into the avenue of Hsiung-nu warriors.

"It's them!" roared Thyrsis. "Roman soldiers!"

11

The lost legion—found!

Could all this be but a dream, wondered Cerdic? Would there be a sudden clap of thunder to awake him in scented grass on Mago's island? His thoughts and those of Festus were one: was it possible that these were the survivors of Carrhae, so many years ago, hundreds and hundreds of miles to the west? Were these the Host of a Thousand, the Warriors with Square Arms, whose exploits had already become a legend from Parthia to the Onion Mountains; who had crossed the vast desert, built this fortification, and now fought in the name of the Merciless One?

The Romans had halted between the escort of torches. Behind a single horseman, more than a hundred foot-soldiers stood at attention.

All eyes were on their leader. He rode a grey stallion. A plume flowed from his helmet. He wore a moulded cuirass—a leather jerkin into which were stitched curved pieces of bronze suggesting the body of a great athlete. He carried a vine staff, the vitis, symbol of his rank of centurion, and across his shoulder he wore a scarlet cloak.

His armour gleamed in the torchlight, but his face remained totally in shadow.

The foot-soldiers wore more simple helmets and the familiar body armour of the legionary, the lorica segmentata. They carried javelins and rectangular shields—the scutum—curved to the shape of the body and embossed with bronze.

The drum-roll was superseded by a single trumpet blast, joined by another, in a fanfare of welcome.

"It's the classicum!" Widuhar's voice was weak with excitement. "Eighteen years it is, since I heard the sound of the cornicines . . . We used to play a fanfare like that when the new commander inspected his troops."

Mago was later to write in his Log that "the very motion of Time seemed to be arrested, and in this curious episode a little-known chapter was added to the book of history". Yet it was to be but the prologue of greater events.

Slowly, the Roman centurion passed down the fire-flickering lines towards the waiting King. A solitary flame leapt across the Roman's face—and Tryphon knew. In his tongueless silence, he forced sound. He croaked. He bleated. He waved his arms and came running to Festus. Hands glasped hands. Eyes transmitted all that needed to be known. "It's him, Tryphon? No doubt?" Tryphon shook his head violently, and all at once there were tears welling out of his eyes, ploughing silver lines through the dust on his cheeks.

As if to take strength from it, Festus kept hold of Tryphon's hand. He looked up. He stared across the darkness, trying to make out the features of the father he had never seen.

He was shaking. For the past months, his life had had one aim. That aim had sustained him through many black days, for he had never doubted that he would find his father. But now he doubted.

Mago divined his thoughts. "Take courage, Festus. It is true, your father may have changed, but he can never forget what he once was."

"He may have no room for me in his heart, Mago,"

responded Festus, his own heart full of dread. "He loved Gaius, my brother. He sent him this ring . . . But Festus! Who is Festus?"

"Stop yer ditherin' an' yer doubtin'," advised Silenos, whose cheery voice soothed the young Roman. "'E's not lyin' on no bed o' roses, i'n't yer father. I mean, look at 'im, 'e's not exactly laughin', is 'e? For t' Fire King's i' trouble . . . Mark my words, yer Dad'll be more'n pleased to 'ave a son fightin' at 'is side."

"There's no love lost between those two," commented Thyrsis as Marinius the Centurion and Jzh-Jzh the Fire King exchanged formal greetings.

"Maybe not," said Widuhar, "but note how even the Merciless One shows his respect for the immortal general of the Host—because he's afraid . . . Yes, that Mars will snatch them back into his celestial armies!"

It was not possible to overhear the discourse between King and Roman, but there was plainly a difference of opinion. Marinius indicated an arc curving north, east and south. He shook his head. He gestured towards his own troops, to the city walls. In turn, Jzh-Jzh pointed proudly at his Hsiung-nu warriors.

He was angry. He refused to listen further. The King had decided. Speak no more on the matter. He dismissed the Centurion, who backed his horse into the Hsiung-nu line to allow the King to pass. He disagreed, but he obeyed.

After Jzh-Jzh came Princess Xandria. She gave Marinius a friendly salute. Here, for sure, was Xandria's tutor in the language of Rome. She paused. She was glancing over her shoulder. She was telling Marinius about Mago and the caravan.

He waited until the King had entered the city. He took a

torch from the hand of one of the last Hsiung-nu. There was silence as he rode out of the mist which had begun to thread gentle spirals through the darkness.

He reined his grey stallion. He stared at the dim faces before him, exhausted, dust-covered, yet aglow with smiles. His rich voice broke the stillness:

"Does Rome live, my friends?"

"Rome lives!" answered Mago. To Tryphon he whispered: "Quickly, go to him."

"Then thrice welcome!" called Marinius, his reserve breaking down at the sight of those he guessed to be his countrymen.

Tryphon stepped into the rim of light. He sped forward and reached for his former master's hand. Momentarily, the Roman responded with a blank stare. Then:

"Tryphon! My Tryphon!" Marinius slipped from his horse. He gathered Tryphon to him in an embrace, lifting him off the ground in delight. "By the Gods, you made it! Speak, my heart's friend. Let me hear you!"

But Tryphon answered by pulling down his lower lip. His forefinger told the story of his silence.

"Your tongue? So the Parthians captured you." Marinius was glancing round. If Tryphon was here, perhaps—Gaius? He gazed at the faces hovering in the mist. "Gaius, my son?" When there was no answer, he looked inquiringly at Tryphon. "You brought my son?"

Tryphon nodded. He led Festus into the torchlight. Unrecognising, father looked on son. "Gaius?" Marinius was forcing himself to recall details of a face which, to his shame, he judged had gone from his memory for ever.

"Not Gaius, father, but Festus." The young Roman's voice was as thin as a blade of grass. He held out the ring of onyx. "I was b-born after you left for Syria."

Marinius did not move. He raised the torch, examining feature by feature this stranger, issue of his own body; and in Festus' stern forehead and determined mouth, Marinius saw himself. "And Gaius? Your mother?"

Festus lowered his eyes.

"Both dead?"

"My Mother, five years ago . . . Gaius and I set out together to search for you." His voice almost deserted him. "I am your only son."

As Cerdic watched this meeting between Festus and his long-lost father, he had a great desire to cry like a baby. He endeavoured to keep back his tears by asking himself why people who were very happy and people who were very sad suddenly had eyes like waterfalls.

Marinius had stretched out his arms, as though sight alone were not enough to convince him that the image before him was real. He touched his son's face, his hair, his shoulders. With gusto and quickening emotion, he embraced him. "I had thought to have no sons, no wife . . . Forgive a poor soldier his loss of words, these womanly tears. But such feelings as flood through me now I never thought to experience again."

He straightened up. His arms were about the shoulders of Festus and Tryphon. "To you all, my hand in friendship. No voyagers ever brought such happiness to a Roman heart . . . Festus, my son, present Marinius the Centurion to the valiant leader who brought you safely across half the world."

As Mago stepped forward, led by Cerdic, and shook Marinius vigorously by the hand, there was a motion behind him. Widuhar had followed, arms open wide. "The Prince of Persepolis, O master, at your service!"

The next few hours were among the most contented Cerdic

had spent on the long journey of exploration. Mago's caravan had been given a rousing welcome by the Roman soldiers. The travellers were plied with hundreds of questions about "how things were back home", and about how they had survived the perils of Parthians, angry river gorges, precipitous mountains, winter snows, bandits and desert. They were also provided with all the food and drink they could consume.

There was lamb, roasted over the open fire of the Roman quarters, juicy shell duck, trout from the Talass and fresh-baked bread seasoned with aniseed.

Cerdic rested against his uncle's Bag of Tricks, well satisfied with his feast. He gazed at the scene around him. Silenos had been right—this was a pimple of a city. Indeed it was nothing more than a village, and scarcely seemed to warrant all the elaborate fortification.

As a last-ditch defence, should the inner wall be successfully stormed, there was an earthen rampart. This was a flat-topped mound some eight feet high skirting a spacious drill-square. It protected the Roman billets on one side of the square and the Fire King's palace—a three-storeyed building of wood and clay-brick—on the other. Beyond were the ramshackle huts of the Hsiung-nu and their families.

King Jzh-Jzh at this moment was feasting with his warriors. Cerdic remembered the dozen or more beautiful women, bedecked in jewels and fine clothes, who had greeted the King on his entry to the city, and especially the tall one, who seemed to command the others. Was she, Cerdic wondered, Xandria's mother? She was similarly dark, with brilliant, fierce eyes.

The shouts and screams of the Hsiung-nu, their dancing and table-drumming, contrasted with the silent rows of Roman faces, illuminated by the camp fire, listening in rapt fascination to Mago.

He spoke of Rome's troubles, of the civil wars that divided the nation as lightning splits an oak, of the attempts of Pompey to become dictator of Rome, and of the murder in the Senate of Julius Caesar.

"Caesar dead!" cried the Romans in dismay.

"Cut down by enemies and friends alike. I am a Carthaginian, yet I weep for Rome's decline. She made good laws and gave a man freedom to speak—all that is gone. Swords answer those who speak up against the powerful. When we left Rome, civil war raged between Antony, Caesar's general, and Octavian, Caesar's nephew. I fear that when you return to your homeland, there will only be tyranny to welcome you."

"Return?" Marinius glanced sadly round at his men. "We shall never return." They nodded their agreement. They knew. "Mago, when you asked me earlier whether the rest of our Roman legion was out on patrol, I laughed, and you detected the bitterness of such a laugh . . . Yet in a way, it is true. Our comrades are out there in the night, forlornly waiting for us to join them in the Kingdom of the Dead.

"Their bodies lie in the desert, under snow and rock, beneath the cold winds of Farghana—fallen from starvation, from exhaustion, from wounds that refused to heal."

Marinius lowered his gaze. "We have no patrols tracking the advance of the armies of the Emperor of Heaven. We are all that remain of those who escaped the Parthians—two hundred out of a thousand!" He raised his arm, and his fist was clenched determinedly. "Yet never have there been warriors like those who have survived—and the Merciless One knows it well!"

As the fire was restored to full brilliance with new logs, Marinius related the adventures of his legionaries since they had been taken into captivity by the Parthians after Carrhae.

Cerdic closed his eyes. He listened, and the events Marinius described formed in his head like vivid pictures on a sunlit wall.

"You will have heard of our disgrace at Carrhae, my friends, of how Crassus led us unwittingly into a trap. And no doubt you will have heard how the Parthians concealed their weapons with coats and skins to deceive us into thinking they were but a bedraggled, poorly-armed force. Over twenty thousand Romans paid with their lives for that mistake.

"When battle commenced, the enemy cast away their disguises. A great blazing light flashed from swords and spears and shields."

"And the banners!" yelled Widuhar. "The Golden Banners!"

"Yes, banners suddenly unfurled, of Seric cloth, beaming in the sun. And the noise! They split the heavens with their shouts, with their hollow-booming drums and their brass bells . . . Then their mounted bowmen came at us like the waves of a wild sea, aiming their shafts at the legs of the Roman infantry, or high in the air so that the very skies were blackened with darts of death.

"No more of that! Suffice it to say that the lucky ones lay dead on the field of battle. Ten thousand of us became prisoners of Surena, the Parthian general."

"Surena!" echoed one of Marinius' men. He spat in the sand. "A painted doll, who had his hair curled by slaves, and had two hundred wagons of wenches and treasure following him."

"That is so," agreed Marinius. "But he was as clever a general as any Roman fought against. When he returned with us to the palace of the Parthian King, Orotes, his reward was—to be executed. Then began years of suffering which even now I cannot look back upon without the drums of anger beating in my heart ... Yet it was anger which helped us survive. Anger alone!

"They packed us into wooden cages beneath the burning sun. There was room only to kneel or stand. They taunted us. They tormented us. They let the wounded die among us, and they left the corpses to rot in our midst. When their drunken feasting began, they took scores—hundreds—from their cages, and used them for archery practice, and made wagers between themselves on how long a Roman could endure, bristling with arrows like a porcupine.

"Their sport done, they put us into the stone quarries. Those who collapsed from exhaustion were taken up to the high cliff and flung down among their comrades below." Marinius paused. He took a drink from his cup of rice wine. He smiled at his son. "Hope, we had surrendered long before but, strangely, the more cruel the Parthians were towards us, the more certain they made our survival. Anger filled us when no food did; and in the depths of winter, as we built roads into the northern mountains, it warmed us.

"For some reason I cannot understand, the Parthians retained intact the wagons full of our arms and armour which Surena had brought to court. They were there for their own use, when necessary, yet perhaps they were also there to tempt us into revolt so that the Parthians could put us to the sword once and for all.

"Each day as I awoke, feeling the shackles around my foot, and the weight of ten hours' stone-carrying still across my back, I saw the wagons. Each day we left the camp, each day we returned, there, as though to remind us of our former selves, were our swords, helmets, shields, javelins. I could not but think that some god remembered us and was generously disposed towards us."

"Mars himself!" cried Widuhar.

"I think you may be right, my friend." Marinius sighed. "For in eighteen years we have known little peace, and little rest. Some of us have been sorely tempted to lay down the sword . . . Yet I rush ahead of myself." He turned cheerfully to Tryphon. "Without the courage and ingenuity of my Freedman here we would have become skeletons in the service of the Parthians.

"One day he found an old spur in the sand. He fashioned it into a key that would unlock our leg-irons and the fetters imprisoning our wrists. The same key released us from our wooden cages. Twice, when the Parthians feasted themselves into drunken oblivion, we planned our escape, and twice the attempt was foiled when the rabble came to seize a dozen prisoners to take part in their brutal party games. They would have us fight lion or be human targets, as I have mentioned.

"On the third occasion, fortune smiled upon us—for a while."

To Cerdic, in his tiredness, the words of Marinius were like stepping stones into a dream. Gradually the words were the dream and the dream-pictures became more real. He saw the cage doors swing open on a starless night. He saw Marinius and fourteen other prisoners crouch in the darkness as Tryphon slid away, key in hand, to the other cages. He saw horses, and behind the horses, shadows. He saw Parthian guards strutting between the horses and the war wagons. The shadows flitted across space. There was a muffled cry, then silence.

His dream was merging with the remembrance of a tale Mago had told him, of how the Greek hero Jason had sown dragons' teeth which sprang up from the field as warriors. The Parthian camp now bristled with Roman warriors, heaving the wagons to safe ground.

Afterwards came the swift journeys with brushwood, with oil. Suddenly Cerdic's dream was aflame as the Parthian camp was aflame. He started up in fright, only to see Mago bending sympathetically over him, and to hear Marinius say:

"Alas, what we had no way of predicting was the arrival of fresh Parthian troops. They rode through the mist at dawn, as many as two thousand of them. Having fought for most of the night, we were forced to enter combat once more. The mountains were behind us; the plain, seething with Parthian archers, before us."

Marinius groaned with the remembrance of that day. "Arrows poured so thickly from the sky that we thought the sun had fallen from the heavens. I can still hear the thud of their points burying into our shields and the cry of our men as they fell.

"Yet we still had our anger—and we were resolved to be slaves no longer. We did not fight for Rome, nor for glory. No orders were given, none taken, and I doubt whether our battle on those green slopes which soon ran with blood will ever be recorded in the history books. But rarely can there have been such a struggle.

"I say no orders were given, and that is true. Yet in our heads there was an order, a command, made—who knows?— perhaps by Mars himself. Surrounded, outnumbered, defenceless against the storm of arrows, we obeyed one order, a single will—we suddenly advanced!"

At these words, Marinius' men cheered and held high their cups.

"Yes my friends, we advanced!" Marinius flushed with

pride. "The Parthians were dumbfounded. While they rocked back on their heels, we thrust straight on to their general and captains, and slew them." Another cheer went up from the Romans. "In those moments, I felt myself and my comrades to be immortal. A million Parthians would not have dislodged us. With every step forward, with every blow struck, our roars of victory grew till they were thunder and lightning in the ears of the Parthians, terrifying them just as their own golden banners had demoralised our troops at Carrhae."

"Aye," whispered Widuhar, "the Golden Banners!"

"At last we learnt that Parthians can flee as speedily as they attack. We avenged Carrhae that day." Marinius' eyes were fire. "Is it to be wondered that afterwards we were said to be invincible, the warriors of the gods?"

"These simple shepherds can confirm that, Master," said Widuhar. "The mere mention of the Host rescued them from certain death in the precincts of my palace at Persepolis."

Marinius emptied his cup. "I am grateful to discover our reputation has brought benefit to others. For us, it has been a curse, pursuing us across time and distance, allowing us no respite from war . . . Sometimes I feel we are like the Greek hero, Odysseus, doomed to wander the world till the gods have pity on us."

"What decided you to march eastwards, to the mountains, Marinius?" Mago wished to know.

"The certainty that the Parthians would re-group and come at us with greater numbers. Of over two thousand Romans who fought on that field without a name, a thousand were killed.

"At first we tracked south along the foothills of the mountains. I was elected commander and immediately despatched Severus, my aid, south and west to try to circle the Parthian encampments and contact Roman forces in Syria; while

Tryphon I sent north, to make the longer journey to my family and home.

"Severus must have been captured and murdered, for Rome learnt nothing of our survival.

"We did not lightly abandon our attempt to find a route west. Yet the whole Parthian nation was set on capturing us, and eventually we were driven into the snow mountains, towards what the native people called the Roof of the World. That first winter was worse than a military defeat. The snows blocked even the lowliest valleys. We huddled in makeshift huts and tents, living off beasts caught in the hunt. Our only wine was the melted snow. The wounded perished in scores, and when spring came, so did the Parthians, pushing us higher and higher into the mountains.

"There is no need for me to describe the horrors of such a journey, for you have experienced them yourselves—but for seven hundred of us to live off such terrain, can you imagine it? Once only did the gods permit us to sheath our swords. We came upon a peaceful valley below the great Onion Mountain. In exchange for the kindness and hospitality of the villagers, we routed the bandit hordes that swarmed from their mountain hideouts to steal crops and cattle, and murder those who endeavoured to stop them."

"There was a few 'as slipped yer net, Marinius," nodded Silenos. "But t'Master put paid to them wi' 'is Bag o' Tricks." He described the avalanche to Marinius.

"I am glad," replied the Roman, "for among those simple people we found peace. We helped till their fields. Many of us being farmers as well as soldiers, we showed them Roman methods of agriculture."

Marinius smiled in happy recollection. "Those were good times. A few of our men thought to settle down in the valleys, marry, forget Rome . . . Yet while there was a single chance left to us to return to our homeland, we knew we must try.

"If Alexander had crossed the mountains and come to the great sea of India, then we could follow his example. Unfortunately there were none among us like Mago the Carthaginian, geographers upon whose memories the lines of land and sea are deeply engraved. The peasant people knew nothing of the world outside their mountains and could not advise us. To the south were snow-capped barriers higher even than those we had traversed. To the east was the desert.

"We tried each in turn, finally following the northward perimeter of the desert."

"So you never crossed the desert, father?" asked Festus.

Marinius shook his head. "Not at that time. We made for the kingdom of Farghana, and received a warm welcome there, for the King was much harassed by the Parthians to the west and the Hsiung-nu to the east. He offered us good pay to fight in his ranks.

"For years I ceased counting, we served Farghana—until the fateful day when the Merciless One led the Hsiung-nu against us. Farghana fell to his fury, as many other nations had done, and we Romans were presented with a simple choice—death, or service with Jzh-Jzh.

"Since then we have breathed nothing but the fire of war. For all his cruelty, the King has treated us with respect, and in the field he is as great a leader as Scipio Africanus or Pompey." Marinius looked about him. "But the evidence is before you . . . two hundred of us are left, many nursing old wounds that have not had time to heal. All of us exhausted with endless warfare.

"Your arrival, Mago, bringing with you my son, has put light into our hearts. We had forgotten Rome, forgotten everything but the task in hand—to fight. And we have fought merely to bring nearer our rest in the Kingdom of the Dead."

He leaned forward, lowering his voice. "That eternal rest is near, my friends." For the space of a minute, he stared into the darkness, with his hand fiercely gripping his son's shoulder as though this alone represented his last hold on sanity and hope.

"You have come at a desperate hour. My son will die alongside his father. All of us will die!"

"Is it really so certain?" asked Mago. "The King boasts that he will burn the cities of the Emperor of Heaven and kill all his people."

Mago's words caused a ripple of bitter amusement among the Romans sitting close by.

"Jzh-Jzh is doomed," said Marinius. "And in his secret thoughts he knows what his fate will be. He boasts. He makes merry with his warriors. In the arms of his beautiful women, he pretends to forget. But even with the blessing of Jupiter and Mars, this frail city cannot withstand forty thousand soldiers of the Emperor of Heaven."

"What is the strength of the King's force?"

"Three thousand—at most."

"Then let him come to terms. Let him make peace."

"Peace! The Merciless One make peace? Never! He scorns the very word . . . And it is too late. The people of the Emperor of Heaven are generous-hearted, lovers of peace—but they will not treat with the Hsiung-nu. Too many promises have been broken by them. Too many acts of treachery perpetrated. Too many innocent victims put to the sword. No, the dragon has come finally upon us, and will consume us in its fire."

Mago refused to give up. "Yet if the Merciless One fights

chiefly to restore his own son, imprisoned by the Emperor of Heaven, surely—"

"Imprisoned? Is that what you have been told? My friend, what has poisoned Jzh-Jzh's heart and wounded his pride beyond mending, is that his wonderful son is a free man! Yes, free—yet he prefers to live among the Seric people rather than return to his own father.

"That is why we fight!"

12

Besieged

Two days had passed. The horizon remained as still and as empty as the desert. At first Cerdic had found himself very much alone. Naturally Festus spent his time with his new-found father. He had been given Roman arms and took part in the daily drill outside the palisades. He accompanied Marinius on his inspection, sharing a solitary vigil, for neither Jzh-Jzh the King nor Torcis his general made a single appearance from the wooden palace; while the Hsiung-nu were in a continual state of drunkenness.

Cerdic was alone, too, because of Mago's illness. His uncle's great strength and endurance had been stretched beyond their limit since the caravan had been captured by the Hsiung-nu. He had begun to suffer terrible head-pains. The slightest movement made them worse. So he lay, like one close to death, in the darkness of the Roman billet. The members of the caravan took it in turns to sit by him.

Then, at last, Cerdic saw the Princess again. She had climbed on to the high platform of the inner wall. She was staring out into the soft evening air. The heaviness in Cerdic's heart vanished. He waited at the foot of the ladder until she looked round.

She smiled. She beckoned him up. She too had found herself alone, unwanted by her father and at odds with the boisterous revelry of the Hsiung-nu warriors. "I hoped I would meet you," she began, simply. "I find that it is your face that comes into my thoughts." She frowned. "When really my thoughts should be of the battle before us."

Cerdic's fingers passed over the strings of his harp. He sighed. "I wonder if I shall ever be able to keep my promise, and teach you to play."

"After my father's victory, then there will be time."

"Three thousand warriors against forty thousand?"

The Princess's eyes flashed angrily. "The sight of one Hsiung-nu can fill a hundred Seric hearts with terror!"

Cerdic was inclined to believe her, and changed the subject. He asked about the King's consort: was she, perhaps . . . Xandria's mother?

The reply came startlingly: "They whisper it over the campfires that my mother died by my father's hand . . . I am forbidden even to mention her name."

They strolled silently along the palisade, feeling an autumn sharpness in the air.

"Look!" Cerdic pointed to the foot of the palisade. Tiny dots of green light hovered above the thick grass. "Fireflies!"

Xandria gave a slight shudder. Her expression changed. "They are unlucky. When the firefly appears, the Bringer of Death is not far behind."

Cerdic laughed quietly. "Then I shall have to cancel your invitation to my uncle's island. There, the night's as full of fireflies as stars. We think they mean good luck." He glanced at Xandria sadly. "Which of us will be proved right?"

He was beginning to see more than the flickering glow of fireflies. He scanned the formerly blank horizon. "Either those are stars fallen from the sky, or they are bonfires. Hundreds of them!"

Xandria was tense with excitement. "Did I not tell you? The fireflies herald the coming of the Emperor of Heaven . . . His campfires return their signals. We must sound the alarm!"

She paused for a second. She wished to say something of importance, something that would preserve their friendship through the coming strife. Instead she slipped from her finger the ring which Mago had used in his "Magic" at Jzh-Jzh's camp. "Wear this for me—and remember Xandria, always!"

She put out her hands to Cerdic. Her fingers closed about his head. She kissed him. Then away she went down the steps from the palisade, calling to the guard in the blockhouse beside the main gates, and shouting "Marinius! Marinius!" across the sandy darkness of the drill-square.

Cerdic remained still. His heart had gone out to Xandria. He felt the old fears, of a boy caught up in the savage world of men, drop from him. Yet new fears replaced them, for Xandria's safety, for the survival of this precious bond of love.

Marinius had answered the Princess's summons immediately. Followed by Festus, he climbed the palisade. "Campfires or fireflies, eh, Cerdic, my lad?"

"Both, I'm afraid, Marinius. The fires stretch as far as you can see."

"How many miles away do you think they are, father?" asked Festus.

"Seven, eight. They are settled for the night, sweet-dreaming on our defeat, I'll warrant." He called to members of his escort below. One had instructions to inform the King; others to rouse the guard in the watch-towers along the palisade. "By first light, they will advance."

Xandria was advised to take rest. "I beseech you, Princess, when the battle begins, do not be tempted to ride alongside your father."

All at once, Xandria ceased to be the girl whose tenderness had been revealed to Cerdic. She reverted to being the true daughter of the Merciless One. "When my father Jzh-Jzh hurls his spear into the cowardly face of the Emperor of Heaven, Xandria will be there to salute his glory!"

She went straight for her horse. She mounted. She glanced back defiantly at Marinius and Festus. To Cerdic she offered a gentle wave of farewell, then spurred her piebald across the drill-square towards the King's palace.

Meanwhile, Widuhar, Thyrsis and Tryphon, with Silenos hesitantly behind, were at the foot of the palisade. "Give us arms, Centurion!" requested Widuhar. "And let your mind be assured as to the outcome of this battle . . . On tomorrow's tide, the royal navy of Persepolis will bring ten thousand of my choicest warriors, with breast-plates forged by Vulcan himself!"

Marinius shouted his thanks. "You, Silenos, are appointed Master Cook to the legion. There'll be Seric gold in your pocket if you keep the stew hot and tasty through the fighting day."

"Aye, well see it don't get flavoured wi'arrers," grinned Silenos. "And there'll be no washin' up till t'battle's over."

"You'll have more than arrows in your stew if you forget to salt it," warned Thyrsis. His eyes gleamed with the prospect of battle. "For my part, Marinius, let me prove my worth as a Roman soldier—and I promise you my sword-arm for life."

Though frequent messages were sent to him, King Jzh-Jzh did not stir from his palace. A simple spoken reply was carried back to his Roman commander: "Not until the dragon marches with two heads shall the Fire King be defeated." Nazir the wizard had re-exerted his influence.

Marinius was successful, however, in hustling the Hsiung-nu warriors into action. They rose from drunken sleep and hastened to man the wooden watchtowers, and to take up their positions along the inner palisade.

After returning to his uncle, and finding him sleeping peacefully, Cerdic joined Marinius and Festus in a tour of inspection. They passed through the gates and the outer palisade to survey the deep-cut trenches.

"Why are they filled with brushwood, father?" Festus inquired.

"An old Roman trick to surprise the Seres. The brushwood conceals sharpened stakes pointing upwards from the ground. We call them Lilies."

They carried on as far as the moat. They paused to look at the Seric bonfires which stretched the entire length of the horizon.

"Have we any chance at at all, Marinius?" Cerdic had never felt such despair.

The Roman centurion turned his gaze on the defended city. "You are no longer children, to be cheered by false hopes. The story of the lost legion ends here ... Those bonfires not only mark the presence of over forty thousand picked troops but of machines of war—catapults and battering rams—which not even the walls of Rome could withstand.

"Jzh-Jzh's allies have deserted him. He has refused to stock up with supplies for a long siege because he is resigned to defeat. Yes, resigned! Never mind what he says about a dragon with two heads."

"Then we've got to surrender," believed Cerdic. "If the Seres are merciful—"

"Jzh-Jzh will as soon surrender as Caesar come back to life." Yet Marinius swished the air determinedly with his vine staff.

"But this I can swear: the Seres will long remember their encounter with the legion that has no name!"

Cerdic was returning to his Uncle Mago in the Roman billet when he saw Torcis and several warriors heading in the same direction. Their arms were full of crossbow parts.

"Y'can't bring that lot in 'ere!" Silenos protested as Torcis entered the billet. "T'master's sick!" He was thrust off his feet.

Cerdic's own protest was ignored. Mago was roughly wakened. He was dragged into a sitting position and the crossbows piled at his feet.

Torcis said nothing. He merely drew a hand, like a knife, across his throat. Mago had been warned. He left one Hsiung-nu warrior inside the billet and one at the entrance.

Cerdic knelt beside his uncle. "Pretend to do it, if you can, Uncle. That is the best way." Mago nodded. His face was ashen white. He found it difficult to breath and occasionally a cough shook his chest as violently as a hunting dog worries its prey.

He grasped Cerdic's hand in his own. "The fever will pass," he whispered hoarsely. "I'm not done for yet, never fear . . . Try to sort the crossbows into separate piles, will you, my boy? . . . And then soothe this old pain-racked head with your music!"

With the first light of morning, a cry went up from the walls, joined by another, then another, repeating the same message: the Seric army was on the march.

Cerdic almost laughed at the eagerness with which the Hsiung-nu guards received this news. They cheered and danced about, waving their spears. Then, heedless of Torcis' commands, they abandoned their prisoner. Thirsty for Seric blood, they raced out into the brightening sunlight.

"Drape the sky with flags!" Marinius had ordered. "Let the enemy *see* we have a military presence here!" Now flags and banners flew from the outer and inner palisades, from the watchtowers and from the King's palace.

The defenders shielded their eyes against the crimson sun which climbed above the helmets of the Seric infantry, still far away.

Before falling back into a deep sleep, Mago had asked Cerdic to reach him his Bag of Tricks. "I want you to try out one of my little inventions." He fished around in the bag for a few moments. "There!" He produced a metal tube about eighteen inches long and an inch in diameter. "Do you remember me grinding the eye-glasses to shape?"

Cerdic ventured out into the drill-square. He tucked "Longsight", as Mago's invention was called, through his belt.

Though the sun was hot, Cerdic was shivering. He felt cold to the marrow of his bones. He watched the preparations for attack. Thyrsis, at work loading a powerful, Roman-style catapult, waved and grinned at him. Tryphon, busy carting stones for the catapult, touched his arm reassuringly before rushing on with his task.

Then Cerdic spotted Widuhar. He was crouched in the shadow of the wall, a hand to his head, stroking the wound he had sustained in the desert. He was whimpering: "My warriors! My warriors, have you betrayed me? How is it that you cannot march until the next full moon? We are lost!"

Cerdic climbed to the platform of the inner palisade. Beyond the moat, Marinius was drilling his legion. Happily among them was Festus. They were advancing in formation, shoulder to shoulder, shield to shield, stopping, breaking line, turning in one direction and then another with the precision of a machine.

Thyrsis spared a second from his endeavours. "That's the famous Roman Testudo they're doing, my boy . . . Who'd ever believe it, thousands of miles away in the wilderness, a formation like that! See how they lock their shields together. The front line's kneeling down, shields on the ground. They are protecting the legs of those behind them."

"Yes, it's like a wall."

"And a roof too, for now look. The third line hold their shields in the air. No other army in the world fights like that."

"It resembles a fishscale," said Cerdic, "But how long will it hold together against the Seric bowmen?"

The armies of the Emperor of Heaven rolled forwards across the plain. They stretched from north to south as far as the eye could see. Cerdic took out his uncle's Longsight. First he saw the bright banners of the enemy—hundreds of them, of Seric cloth gleaming majestically. Longsight enabled him to detect even the motifs on the banners: green dragons, winged dragons inscribed in gold, a snake and tortoise, a red bird and a white beast he could not recognise.

He saw the ranks of bowmen, and between each bowman marched a spearman. Helmets and breastplates shone. Spear tips glimmered like stars. At intervals rode the cavalry, heavily armoured, with long lances and round, brilliantly painted shields.

Between bowmen and cavalry came the machines of war—catapults, rams, climbing towers. Cerdic blinked in the sunlight. He rubbed his eye and gazed once more through Longsight. "They're even bringing their own walls with them!" he exclaimed. "Decorated with dragons." He was glad to see that none of the dragons had two heads.

Cerdic turned at the shouts behind him. King Jzh-Jzh had at last deigned to recognise the impending battle. Clad in his familiar red leather, he now wore breastplates (taken from a Seric general whom Jzh-Jzh personally had beheaded) and a Roman helmet with a scarlet plume.

He was surrounded by the women of his household, clad in Sericum. Some wept, some pressed their affections upon him, until he dismissed all of them save his consort—and Princess Xandria who came galloping through the crowd, spear held high.

Cerdic groaned in anguish. Xandria wore neither helmet nor armour. Her only protection was a round shield slung over her shoulder. Her hair was bunched under a black leather cap.

The drill-square seethed with Hsiung-nu warriors impatient to break out from the confines of the city and drive the Seres back across the plain. They cheered their king as he leapt on to his horse of Farghana. A quiver of spears hung at his side. Through his belt was a Roman broad-sword.

Two days of carousing, far from exhausting him, had renewed him. He was aflame with energy, and the heat of it warmed the hearts of his warriors. They felt his power. When he raised his spear and shrieked the Hsiung-nu cry of battle, they roared back with joy.

The great gates between the watchtowers were open. Inside the city were the jubilant Hsiung-nu, outside were the silent ranks of the two hundred Romans.

The Merciless One addressed them all. "Jzh-Jzh will not cease the song of battle till the grass turns red with the blood of the Emperor of Heaven and his people. Not till the Wall of the

Giants lies a heap of rubble at my feet, and the mothers of the Seric nation weep for their losses.

"There will be no treaty, no peace—no prisoners! We give no quarter, and we ask for none. Thus will my son be avenged! Take courage, my friends, from what has been predicted: none but a dragon with two heads will triumph over the Fire King!" His spear challenged the sky. He yelled the order to advance.

The Hsiung-nu swept through the city gates. So eager were they to reach the approaching armies, that several fell headlong into the angled trenches. Others rode straight into—and out of—the deep moat, as if nothing in the world but an arrow through the heart could stop them.

Cerdic waved to Xandria. He shouted. But she was gone, her horse matching the King's stride for stride.

Jzh-Jzh's onslaught against the front ranks of the Seric bowmen and spearmen was heroic. His warriors attacked in a mad, undisciplined rush. They shrieked, they howled. They split the air as much with their laughter as their spears. They forced the neat Seric lines asunder. They hurled in among them, hacking and thrusting.

Cerdic tried desperately to keep Longsight fixed upon Xandria's position. It was impossible. One instant he saw her, the next she was hidden in the mass. He glanced towards the Romans. They remained in the rear, alert and still.

The Seric advance had been arrested, but there was no retreat, only a confusion of flashing spears, bodies falling, horses rearing, and the din of spear on shield, sword on sword, the swish of arrows and the startled, agonised cries of the wounded.

While the Hsiung-nu had made an inroad on the central flank of the Seric army, they had no answer for the lines of bowmen to right and left. Protected by bristling rows of spears,

the bowmen took aim, holding their fire until a single order
was given.

The effect of their volleys, shot diagonally from two directions, was devastating. Hsiung-nu warriors dropped from their
horses like forest saplings before the axe. Those following
rushed straight into riderless horses, lost control and were
helpless before the second volley.

Still Jzh-Jzh drove them on, his scarlet figure darting from
side to side behind the main battle area. Xandria rode boldly
by his side. Her shield had three arrows buried in it.

Jzh-Jzh permitted not a yard of retreat. Those warriors who
dared turn their horses round faced impalement upon their own
comrades' spears, and were forced back into the range of the
crossbows.

Now the kneeling Seric infantrymen rose. As one man they
marched several paces forward.

"The line's breaking!" Cerdic felt sick with fear for Xandria.

Another volley of arrows, another advance of the infantry,
and the Hsiung-nu began to give ground. There was no way
out for their terrified horses. One way spears, the other,
arrows.

Again Cerdic lost sight of Xandria. He put Longsight to his
eye. He saw a Hsiung-nu go down with an arrow in his face.
He saw a Seric bowman stumble headless among tangled
bodies. And he saw Xandria—surrounded. She fought as
bravely as her father, then all at once, she was no longer there.
Cerdic gasped. He could see the Princess's piebald horse:
riderless.

"She's hit!"

Thyrsis was next to him. "Let me look!" He tore
Longsight from Cerdic's grasp. "The King's seen her. Mars
himself would envy such a warrior!"

Cerdic had no need of Longsight. He could see well enough the furrow Jzh-Jzh had driven, single-handed, through the Seric infantry. Three men, four men, fell to his sword and spear. Another he kicked aside, another his horse trampled under foot.

"He's got her!" shouted Thyrsis. "She's hit, lad—badly!" He thrust Longsight back into Cerdic's hand. "See for yourself . . . They'll none of them get out of that lot alive."

Cerdic raised Longsight again. He saw the veiled face of Jzh-Jzh spattered with blood. He saw him reaching down into the turmoil of bodies. He was pulling Xandria across his horse.

There was an arrow in her back.

The King was alone. The other Hsiung-nu were either galloping or running away towards the city moat. Cerdic himself was running. He had leapt down the steps of the palisade in threes. He slipped out of the main gates.

"Marinius! Marinius!" he shouted, making for the Roman ranks which were still in defensive order.

From their position on the ground, the Romans had only a restricted view of what was happening beyond the rear line of the Hsiung-nu attack.

"Marinius!" Cerdic dodged among the retreating Hsiung-nu. "Xandria's fallen, and the King is cut off."

With a glance at his son Festus, the Roman centurion signalled for a troop of fifty men to follow him. Cerdic was left stranded. He saw a stray horse coming towards him. He reined it. He mounted.

There was no time for thinking. None for doubting. He had a sword. He would use it. So he galloped forward, keeping close to Festus. He heard the whistle of a crossbow bolt. He felt the breath of another.

For the first time in history, the warriors of Rome and those of the Emperor of Heaven met in combat. The disciplined Romans took the Seres by surprise. They caused the advance to waver. The tight Seric lines opened up and King Jzh-Jzh, with his wounded daughter lying limply over his horse's neck, came riding through.

And when they retreated, the Romans moved in order, forming solid walls of shield and spear against the numberless opposition. Cerdic was boxed in among them. He was beside the King, his eyes on Xandria. She had been pierced in the lower part of the back. She was bleeding profusely.

There was one name on the Fire King's lips as he passed through the great gates. "The Blind One!" he cried. "Bring the Blind One, for he alone will I trust with my daughter."

Cerdic ran from his horse. He stood in front of the King. "My uncle is sick with fever, and exhausted, My Lord—but he has taught me the arts of surgery and medicine."

With the help of Marinius and Festus, the King had lowered Xandria to a rug placed on the ground. "You? A mere boy!"

"The gods have filled his hands with the gift of healing, My Lord," said Festus. "He has proved it."

The King stooped over his daughter. All the ferocity of battle had gone out of him. He shook his head. He looked upward in the sunlight towards Cerdic. "She has spoken well of you . . . Save her life. I beg you. And earn the fathomless gratitude of a king."

13

Fulfilment of a prophecy

The moment Cerdic had begun to uncover Xandria's wound, his uncle awoke. Light from the torch held by Silenos shone on Mago's pallid face, streaming with sweat. He heaved himself on to his elbow, then sat up.

"The Princess has been hit, Uncle. The arrow's still in her back."

"Let me examine her." Mago dragged himself over to where Xandria lay on her side. His fingers now were his only eyes.

"We must staunch the blood, Uncle!"

Mago nodded. "But first the arrow will have to be removed." As though he could see Cerdic, he gazed hard at him. "My boy, I've never asked you to do anything as difficult as this . . . But my own blind hands—"

"I'll do it. Anything to save her!"

Thyrsis came rushing in with the news. "The Romans have formed the Testudo, out there beyond the moat. They've gained a hundred yards or more, and held it."

Cerdic unwrapped Mago's kit of medicines and surgical instruments. He selected a small saw-blade. Following his uncle's instructions, he began to sever the arrow-point that protruded from Xandria's side. He cut at a downward angle to reduce vibration and avoid enlarging the wound.

A trickle of sweat ran from his hair to his eyes. He was about to raise his hand to wipe the sweat away. But the hand was red with Xandria's blood.

"If she should die, Uncle . . ."

"Keep your mind on your task!" rapped Mago. He had moved forward on his knees. He held Xandria firmly. "Now!"

Slowly, not daring to breath, gently, his hand quivering ever so slightly, Cerdic withdrew the arrow.

"Well done, my boy!" Mago immediately clamped two wads of cloth, soaked in wine-spirit, against the wound.

His instructions for bandaging Xandria were almost drowned by a massive roll of drums from the enemy lines.

The Romans, in Testudo, had never heard such a concerted sound—not even at Carrhae. "There must be ten thousand drums!" shouted Festus to his father.

"Romans hold firm!" ordered Marinius.

The Seres were hauling forward their huge, wooden walls or shields. Covering fire was provided by the bowmen. The air darkened with their arrows. The hum of the bolts that tore through the Roman shields was terrifying. One sliced the back of Festus' hand. A second struck below the centre of his shield and split it from top to bottom.

There was no respite from the arrows, for each bowman had his own loader who thrust another ready-primed bow into his hands the instant he had fired the first. Festus noticed how the loaders dropped deftly on to their backs, holding the bows firmly with their feet as they pulled the string and bolt into position.

Still maintaining their Testudo formation, the Romans retreated over the moat. The plank bridge was dragged away. Several fell under the hail of arrows as the legionaries sprinted between the lily trenches.

In the Roman billet, Cerdic had finished bandaging

Xandria's wound. He scarcely heard Mago's compliment: "You did an excellent job, Master Surgeon." He stared at the Princess, willing her to revive.

"She's so pale, Uncle! Her skin was brown like the sand, and now . . . it's whiter than the scarf around her throat."

"There is nothing further we can do," replied Mago, with a a tremour in his voice, "but keep her warm—and above all, keep her still."

The Romans had passed through the outer, unmanned, palisade, then under the great gateway of the city. The inner palisade was thick with defenders. They were waving their javelins, swords and longbows and trying to outshout the roar of the Seric drums.

The gates were locked. Marinius gave the order for the catapults to be fired as soon as the Seres reached the outer palisade. Cauldrons of oil were simmering on iron braziers stoked with dung. There were piles of rocks to be cast upon the armoured battering rams of the enemy, should they get as far as the inner palisade.

The Seric artillery was already within shooting range. Missiles came heavy-thudding against the palisade, or twisting through the air and burying into the banks of the earthen rampart.

Torcis, the King's general, shrugged when he was asked by Marinius where his master was. He gestured towards the palace. "Retired?" exclaimed the Roman. "In the very teeth of battle, he seeks refuge in the arms of his consort?"

Marinius translated Torcis' explanation for Festus. "Jzh-Jzh is ashamed to fight with warriors who deserted him. He refuses to set eyes on Torcis again until he returns from a triumphant attack . . . Very well, Torcis, the command of the gate is yours. Yet heaven help those who ride with you!"

Smarting under his King's accusation, Torcis gathered about him a hundred of his special braves. He ordered the gates to be opened. Out there advanced an army of such might that a thousand men under a wise general would have hesitated before attacking. But with shrill cries of vengeance the Hsiung-nu charged forward. They soared over the trenches. A few even leapt the moat while the rest plunged in, causing sheets of spray to sparkle around them.

Torcis led them on. They wheeled round the great shields. They hacked down those who dared block their passage. They forced back the front line of Seric bowmen. All was confusion. Metal jarred on metal. Arrows flew. Spears struck home.

For a few moments it seemed that Torcis' valiant attack had dislodged the entire centre column of the Seric army. There were signs of panic in the rear ranks as well as those that bore the brunt of the Hsiung-nu attack.

Torcis swept on, cutting a swathe of space. Archers, spearmen, cavalry fell before him. But the Hsiung-nu were forcing a passage to nowhere. The way behind them filled with Seric spearmen. They were enveloped.

Yet it did not matter to them. They fought as though only victory could result from their endeavours, until one by one they were dragged from view into the mass of Seric spears. Last to go was Torcis. Streaming with blood, he still jabbed and thrust with a broken spear, ignoring the crossbow bolts which showered into him.

All at once he was gone, swallowed up by wave after wave of infantry who now pressed forward to the moat, which Seric engineers had already begun to drain.

In the calm of the Roman billet, Xandria opened her eyes. She tried to speak but could only whisper: "I fought well? . . .

Did you see me?" Cerdic held her hand, while Mago stroked her brow.

"Lie quietly, Princess. You must conserve all your strength."

Her smile was strange, distant. "Soon I shall have strength enough." She fought for breath. "Do you remember the fireflies, Cerdic?"

"Please, Xandria, rest!"

"I think that . . . I was proved right."

Cerdic felt his throat swell, his eyes prick. "No, no! We'll have that horse-race together. To the lake of salt and back!"

Mago's steadying hand was on Cerdic's arm. "Let the Princess sleep."

Thyrsis carried in an order from the wall. "Marinius is calling everyone who can lift a spear to join him in the defences. Not you, Silenos," he said, as if the fat cook had stirred himself to move—which he hadn't. "But with your permission, Master, I'll set myself among them. Widuhar is there, and Tryphon."

Mago sensed the grief mounting in Cerdic's heart, and he understood why the boy pleaded to go out and fight on the wall. Only action would stifle his fears for Xandria. "Very well," Mago agreed. "You may go, but only to bring back messages from the wall. We shall need to be ready to move the Princess at any moment."

Because of the Lily trenches, the Seres had to leave behind their mobile walls. They came for the outer palisade with fiercely burning torches that wreathed the faces of the infantry-men in smoke.

Marinius controlled the defenders' fire. His arm was raised. Arrows were drawn, spears poised, catapults loaded and in position. Down came his arm.

The volley riddled the front ranks of the attackers. Yet the advance continued. The Seres reached the outer palisade. They had brought brushwood with them. They stacked it against the palisade, and their torches were thrust into action.

The drums boomed ceaselessly across the battlefield. There was the clang of heavy bells—and suddenly the whispering approach of a new weapon.

Balls of fire soared into the smoke-tracered sky. They hung in the air. Then they crashed at the foot of the walls, on to the platform, into the sand. And as the Seres consolidated their position, bringing up their artillery behind their mobile walls, the fire-balls struck farther into the city.

Helpless, terrified, fraily protected by a shield he had taken from a fallen Hsiung-nu warrior, Cerdic watched the fire-balls dropping nearer and nearer the Roman billet.

One ball spluttered and exploded at the very entrance, but its sparks were doused by the cloud of sand it had stirred up.

The fire-balls multiplied in number, followed by lighted arrows. Soon their range would take in the wooden palace itself.

The Seric infantrymen were no more the remote figures Cerdic had brought into view with Mago's Longsight. They were thirty yards away, sprinting under volleys of arrows. They were at the foot of the inner palisade itself, heedless of the oil that cascaded, scalding, over them, dying, but in the process, stacking the wall with brushwood.

"We're alight!" cried Festus. He was holding out a skin bucket to Cerdic. "We've got to put the fires out . . . There's water on the platform. But watch your head!"

Cerdic felt dizzy. So far he had kept his head below the level of the spiked wall. He had watched arrows screaming over it. He had seen men fall, hit in the face—and now he was asked to look over that wall, locate the rising fires and direct water over them. It was madness!

He could hear two poundings, one of arrows striking the palisade, the other of blood pumping through his frightened heart.

"Hurry up!" called Festus who seemed oblivious to arrows and fire-balls.

Cerdic was forced to rise, his shoulder hard against the wall. He counted five. Then, with the swiftest glance that ever took place, he tipped his water over the palisade and ducked down again. He scrambled along to the trough to refill his bucket. At the same moment, looking up, he saw the arms of a scaling ladder.

"Festus! They're coming up!"

His friend was beside him. "Help me push it away!"

Cerdic's mouth opened. He swallowed. He felt Festus' strength go out, heaving at the ladder. He couldn't manage it alone. "Please, Cerdic!" He was up too. He could see the whole battlefield, the fire-balls, the faces of infantrymen picking a way between the Lily trenches, the heads of those attempting to set the walls aflame—and he could see the soldier mounting the scaling ladder.

It was too heavy. He was trying. His hands were on the ladder, but it was too heavy. A second infantryman was climbing it. Festus reached for his sword. Cerdic looked about him. He picked up a fallen spear. It shook in his hand. There was blood on it. He watched Festus. He waited as he did. "Now!" The order came only dimly to him. But he raised his spear. He closed his eyes. He jerked his weapon downwards. He heard a cry. The spear slipped past metal into something soft. Then its point was free.

"Well done lad!" Marinius' voice carried along the line.

Festus had leaned out. Together they pushed the empty scaling ladder sideways. It fell into the fires that were licking hungrily at the wall.

There was one brief pause in the fighting. The Seres checked their next onslaught until the terrific heat from the fire consuming the outer palisade had abated.

Dusk had begun to spread over the land. Without the rivalry of the sun, the fires burnt more brightly.

"Will they withdraw for the night, do you think, father?" asked Festus.

Marinius wiped the sweat from his forehead. "They will turn this city into a mound of ash before dawn." He was on the move, leaping down from the platform. He commanded a small side gate in the wall to be opened and, with three of his legionaries, he sped forward, returning instantly with a wounded Seric infantryman.

At the same time King Jzh-Jzh stepped from his palace. His scarlet tunic and armour shone with an unearthly glow. A bonfire had been lit by Nazir the wizard in the centre of the drill-square. He commenced to dance round it, flinging handfuls of salt into the flames. He chanted. His bones rattled. He abased himself before the King.

Yet Jzh-Jzh was more interested in Marinius' captive. He was proud again, defiant. "Would you have the slave run back to plead on our behalf for mercy?" His voice resounded across fire and sand and darkness.

"He has given us information, My Lord," answered Marinius.

"The Merciless One requires no information from a Seric slave." Jzh-Jzh smiled behind his veil. "Does he tell you how many Seric mothers weep for those Jzh-Jzh has slain these many years past? Does he tell you of the merchants I have robbed, the houses I have burned—and the messengers of peace whose heads I have returned on spears? One question you may ask him: why is the Emperor of Heaven so foolish that he sends his soldiers to die at the hands of one who can only be defeated by the dragon with two heads?"

Marinius did not reply.

"Answer me, what does he say?"

Marinius spoke hesitantly. "My Lord, the prophecy may well be true. For if the army of the Emperor of Heaven is represented by a dragon, then it does indeed have two heads."

"Impossible!"

"Two generals, My Lord, of equal rank, lead the Seric armies. They are called Gan and Tang, young men taking their first joint command."

King Jzh-Jzh seemed not to have heard. But he turned. He kicked the kneeling Nazir away from him. He held out his hand. A spear was placed in it. Then he gave the Hsiung-nu cry of victory. Followed by his men, he raced to the palisade just as the next great attack of the Seric army began.

Brushing past Festus and Cerdic, the King strode forwards and backwards along the platform, in full view of the enemy, haranguing them, challenging them to do their worst.

His action put new courage into the defenders. But it also caused the attackers to concentrate their men and resources. It was as though the entire army had been commanded to aim at one man, and Jzh-Jzh's dazzling scarlet tunic made a sharp-etched target against the darkness.

Once more came the fire-balls, like meteors bursting from the sky; once more the Seric infantry stoked up the fires at the foot of the city wall. The bowmen's arrows cut invisibly through the air, by their very impact sending the defenders stumbling from the platform.

Cerdic heard the terrifying sound of scaling ladders—hundreds of them—being pushed into position. He was glad Festus was fighting farther along the wall and would not see how his friend crouched down, how he would rather leap from the platform than raise his head again to view the oncoming infantry.

His eyes were on King Jzh-Jzh. What bravery he showed in comparison to Cerdic's! He was suddenly like a god. The arrows and the spears sprayed round him, yet he remained untouched. He was fighting with spear and sword at the same time. One after another, the climbing infantrymen fell back into the pit of darkness and fire as Jzh-Jzh severed their arms, their heads or speared them with savage thrusts.

Gradually the pressure of the Seric attack forced the Hsiung-nu king and the Roman centurion together. Shoulder to shoulder they fought.

"I regret nothing!" roared the King. "And I shall die regretting nothing. Do you hear, Marinius? The Seres will tell their grandchildren and their great grandchildren till the ending of time of this day! They will spin a thousand tales of the Fire King and his Invincible Romans. And we shall live as none of their emperors will live!"

Cerdic sprang away from the wall. It was hot now, smouldering from the fires below. He rose. The infantrymen were coming over the top. One of them aimed straight for him. He felt a spear pinion his shield. Another was coming at him.

"Fight!" cried Festus rushing up from behind and saving Cerdic from a blow he did not see and could never have parried. Tryphon was there. He brought down one man, then a second, while Widuhar was on the steps leading from the platform, firing a long-bow whenever a head appeared above the wall.

Repulsed, the attackers fell back. They were replaced by fresh troops, and another tide of destruction beat against the burning palisade.

Then, all at once, the Fire King grunted. He reeled sideways and but for Marinius' steadying arm he would have fallen from the platform. A shot from a crossbow had struck him in the face. His knees folded under him. His sword clanged on to the wooden boards, slipped over the edge and quivered in the sand below.

The King refused to be carried from the battle. He wrenched the bolt from his face. He ignored the blood which spurted through his veil and over his scarlet tunic.

Along with the Seric bolt, Jzh-Jzh had torn away the veil. Cerdic saw that terrible face for the first time. Yet the King's eyes were Xandria's eyes. He was up. He held the veil to the wound. And with his other hand, he fought.

"To the death, my warriors! Show the Seres that the wounded lion fights more fiercely than ever!"

By this time the watchtowers were ablaze, the defenders fleeing from them. The great gates were bulging inwards under the force of the Seric battering rams.

Cerdic had come down from his position on the wall. His only concern was for Mago and Xandria. The fires would soon spread to the billet, if the fire-balls did not set it alight sooner. They were pitching all round it. Store sheds, barns and then the stables were aflame.

Terrified horses broke down the doors and streamed in panic across the drill square, swerving and bucking as arrows and fire-balls dropped in their path.

Another fire billowed into the sky—the King's palace was alight and women and slaves fled from it in all directions.

"Does she hold her own, Uncle?" asked Cerdic kneeling beside Xandria.

"She breathes." Mago gently pulled a blanket over the Princess's shoulder.

"But will she live?"

Mago listened to the battle ranging ever nearer. "Will any of us live, my boy?"

With no need to show a brave face, Cerdic sought refuge in his uncle's arms. They ignored the fire arrows that struck the billet, for the freshly-stripped logs of the wall charred but did not set alight.

"Mercy on us!" Silenos had crawled on hands and knees to the door of the billet. "Master, they're over t'wall!"

Thyrsis was back, his eyes aglow with the relish of battle. "I'll think no more ill of that warrior," he panted. "The Fire King's just ordered the gates open—as if they needed opening! With his consort right by him, he's led out an attack. And what an attack!—he's cleared the palisade."

"Aye, but what about them 'as came over t'top?"

"Trapped by Marinius and his boy. There'll be laurels for Festus if we survive this day . . . I am to remain here on guard, Master."

Jzh-Jzh's lightning charge into the ranks of the Seric infantry bought time. He forced a withdrawal. He chopped the ladders from the wall—but the wall was already ablaze. The gates were gone and so was the last of the King's strength.

He saw nothing of his consort's brave death. His scarlet tunic drenched with blood, he had to be held on his horse. Yet he managed to ride back into the city. He fell into the midst of his faithful Hsiung-nu. He was carried to a part of the palace which had not been destroyed by fire.

With a roll of drums and an unearthly jangle of bells, the

Seres resumed their offensive. An instant later, two fire-balls lodged in the capsized roof of the billet. The roof smouldered. Then it was in flames.

Marinius' shrill cry went out for the legionaries to assemble. "Abandon the wall!" They came wounded, bleeding, with battered shields, broken spears and swords. There were still over a hundred of them.

The last position that could be defended was the earthen rampart. Festus and Tryphon were despatched to assist Mago and the rest to carry Xandria into the open. The billet was a furnace.

Forestalled by the men from helping to carry Xandria, Cerdic turned to take his uncle's arm. But Silenos was already leading him towards the earthen rampart.

Alone, Cerdic remembered precious things. He ignored Marinius' order for the unarmed to shelter behind the Roman line. He dashed back to the billet.

Through the smoke, through the fire, Cerdic could see a way in. He took a deep breath. He headed in between the swirling flames. Timbers crashed around him. His eyes were streaming, burning with the smoke, but there was no need to go looking. He was bursting for breath. He stooped into the dark.

He emerged, arms full; coughing, and not knowing his tunic was ablaze. Festus raced towards him as if he intended to punish him for disobedience. Instead, he threw him to the ground. He rolled him in the dust and sand until the fire was put out.

"That was madness!" he cried, dragging Cerdic behind the wall of Roman shields.

"I just had to get my harp! It's going to be a gift for Xandria when she is better." He coughed. He was proud of what he had done and he knew Festus was not really angry with him.

"And how could I let Mago's Log, and his Bag of Tricks, be destroyed?"

Over the palisade came the Seric infantry. Through the gates galloped the Seric cavalry, slaughtering those Hsiung-nu who dared to stand and fight, and pursuing those that fled.

"Make Testudo!" commanded Marinius. The Roman shields locked against attack on all sides, and against the continuing hail of arrows and artillery from above.

Cerdic crouched down, gripping Mago's Bag of Tricks with one hand, his harp with the other. He saw Tryphon had fallen, struck through the heart, and he saw boyish tears burst into Festus' eyes. He saw his Uncle Mago arching his body, like a shield, over the Princess. And he saw the last territory of the Fire King's empire diminish inch by inch.

Yet the Roman Testudo held. Wave after wave of the Seric infantry was repulsed. The cavalry was no more successful. Though the Seres had taken the city, though the city was aflame from end to end and the dead lay scattered in hundreds—and most thickly around the feet of the defenders—the Testudo resisted.

Dawn rose on a scene of horrifying devastation—a city razed to ugly black stumps, the ground a lake of blood. In the centre of that lake stood an island of Roman shields.

Throughout the night Cerdic had knelt beside Princess Xandria. Her hand was locked tightly in his. Her eyelids flickered. She breathed fitfully, occasionally emitting a whimper of pain.

Suddenly, Cerdic realised that the battering of spears and arrows and swords and stones and fire-balls, had ceased. He peered up. He could not believe it.

Silence.

He could hear the wind again. Between the bleeding legs of

the Roman legionaries, firm as pillars on the earth, he saw a leaf. A leaf! Carried by the breeze, its delicate veins transfigured by the sun. How beautiful! How miraculous!

And across the beautiful silence came a horseman, commander of cavalry. He wore a blue uniform richly decorated with gold. Cerdic looked away in revulsion, for the horseman held aloft the head of Jzh-Jzh the Fire King.

When Cerdic glanced back, the head was gone. Now he saw flags and pennants of shining Sericum. He saw bright-stitched emblems—dragons of gold, dragons of green, the snake and tortoise, the red bird. And he saw the charging form of a white tiger.

Except for the fluttering pennants, there was no movement from the assembled Seric army. Marinius had lowered his shield. He stood up. He waited for the Seric commander to speak.

To Cerdic, it seemed a long speech, but with every word, his hopes grew. His heart leapt when Marinius translated what the commander had said.

"His name is Du Hsun. He requires us to surrender to the mercy of the Emperor of Heaven ... We are to be spared, friends! Our valour this day has won honour in the eyes of the Seric nation."

Du Hsun was speaking again. This time Marinius' face darkened. He was slow to translate. He turned to look at Mago, still shielding the Princess. "He says that all shall live save the daughter of the Fire King, whose body has not been found in the palace."

Cerdic trembled. His head was reeling. He heard Festus whisper to his father, "Then we must fight on."

There was another silence. The breath of the soldiers filled the cold morning air. Cerdic had his arm protectively round Xandria, and his uncle's arm was around him.

Then, something was missing. Cerdic no longer felt the squeeze of Xandria's fingers through his. They were relaxed, loose. He looked down at her and let out a cry of despair.

Mago was gathering her up in his arms. Swayingly, with Silenos' help, he got to his feet. Tears had begun to glisten on his cheeks.

"The Princess," he announced in a broken voice, "now flies with her father to the Kingdom of the Dead. May the gods bless her short life!"

Conclusion

Over a year had passed. It was spring again, and on the green slopes running up from the great Wall of the Seres, there was a sprinkling of white jonquils and purple crocus. From the hills, the Wall swooped into the far valley. Then it climbed, snake-like, to the distant snowline and vanished into mountains and sky. Gentle puffs of smoke floated up from the watchtowers.

The Wall had not known such peace for a generation.

Thoughts, feelings, memories tumbled over one another in Cerdic's mind as he looked out at the land of the Seres for the last time. He watched the holiday crowds streaming towards the Wall from their salmon-roofed villages. They were as-sembling for a very important ceremony.

Usually so bleak and forbidding, guarded by silent troops for ever scanning the misty plains for the advance of the Hsiung-nu, the Great Wall now shone along its whole visible length with flags. Some flew from the towers, some were held by Seric infantry on the wall itself, but most were waved by hordes of bright-clad children.

Westwards from the Wall, Marinius' Roman legionaries, their arms polished till they gleamed like fire in the morning sun, stood at attention—145 of those who had escaped the Parthians after Carrhae. They were to be awarded a singular honour from the Emperor of Heaven.

Festus was among them, and Thyrsis who, with Mago's blessing, had fulfilled a lifetime's dream—to become a Roman soldier. Soon they would be saying their goodbyes. Mago's caravan, heavy-laden with Seric merchandise (and to Widuhar's delight, rolls and rolls of shining Sericum) was ready to begin the homeward journey.

Cerdic's despair at the death of Xandria had battered him as violently as the mountain gorge pounds the rocks in its path. In those dark days he left boyhood behind him. Now his grief was more like the Talass river, part of the map of his life, yet gently flowing. On his finger, he wore Xandria's ring; around his throat was her scarf of white Sericum. He looked out, and he felt he could see her, galloping wildly across the plain.

He was remembering what Mago had said: "She was a flower of the battlefield. Nothing could have changed her. Peace would have been a desert to her, and withered her. Treasure her as she was, not what she might have been!"

There was sadness too in Cerdic's heart at the thought of never seeing Festus again, or this wonderful country which no westerner had ever visited before.

But he drew comfort from the happy prospect of returning to Carthage, with the treasure he carried at this moment tightly under his arm: Mago's Log. "Can there ever have been a book like this!"

It told the story of an empire unknown to Rome, recording in exact detail the Seric way of life. When Cerdic closed his eyes, he saw the visions which Mago's Log described: the sumptuous palace of the Emperor, the pleasure gardens, the plashing fountains, the bustling markets, the forests of towers built for heavenly observation. He saw carriages glittering with silver and gold, horses caparisoned with breastplates and pendant jewellery, street jugglers, performing animals, sword-dancers.

The memories were not only in his eyes but in his ears. He heard bells and drums, flutes and fifes. He heard the chant of choirs from rich men's windows, and his own attempts to play the three-stringed zither and the lyre.

Yet the memory Cerdic knew he would cherish most was the welcome his Uncle Mago had received from the scholars and scientists of the land. Word of this explorer and inventor spread before him wherever he went. Eventually he was offered a privilege never before granted to a foreigner—an audience with the Emperor of Heaven himself.

From then on, Mago had been a celebrity. The whole of Seric science and discovery was open to him, though one secret was kept even from him. Only Widuhar was really disappointed at this, for it was the method by which Sericum was manufactured.

The ceremony was about to begin. Cerdic went down from the wall to join Mago waiting at the head of the caravan. Silenos, fatter than ever after a year of Seric feasts, was beside him. "I'm goin' to miss them quales wi' oranges, Master, and them roast piglets stuffed wi'pickle."

On the summons of a deep-throated gong, columns of Seric cavalry rode through the gates of the Great Wall. They were led by the "Two-headed dragon", General Gan and General Tang. Directly behind came Colonel Du Hsun, carrying a furled banner.

Cerdic described the scene to his uncle: "Marinius is coming to meet them, proud as one of those statues in the Roman Forum . . . Yet who but us will know of his deeds?"

"Marinius' noblest work lies ahead of him," replied Mago.

"And one thing is certain, the Testudo that saved our lives will be immortalised."

"How, Uncle?"

"Thanks to Marinius, the Seres have adopted a Roman custom. An artist will record the triumph of the Emperor of Heaven over the Fire King. He will paint a scene of each phase of the battle, so that the wall of Roman shields that withstood a whole army, will be remembered for ever."

Marinius and the Seric generals had met. The Roman centurion raised his vine staff in salute. Now Colonel Du Hsun came forward. He unfurled the Seric banner.

The red-dyed flag shimmered in the spring breeze. Its emblem, in blazing white, was that of the tiger.

"That's the flag I saw in my vision!" cried Widuhar. "A white tiger!"

"The Tiger of the West," explained Mago, "protector of the western lands, just as the Red Bird guards the south, the Snake and Tortoise the north and the Green Dragon the east."

General Gan took the banner. He held it high in the wind. Then he presented it to Marinius. There was cheering from the Seric ranks, which faded as the General spoke.

"By the express wish of the Emperor of Heaven, Lord of the Seric Peoples," he announced, "as a tribute to your valour, and in accordance with the treaty agreed between us, we name you the Legion of the White Tiger. We assign you the task of defending, in perpetuity, the western approaches to His Imperial Majesty's kingdom. And by this token we welcome you as citizens of His Heavenly Empire!"

Cheers went up from the crowd. Flags were waved. The Seric troops joined in with shrill hurrahs.

"In addition," continued Gan as the applause died away, "the Emperor has commanded that the Legion of the White

Tiger shall live not as pressed men, but as governors of their own city, the building of which will be financed from the Royal Purse."

The General paused. He smiled. "And the name of that city shall be Li-Jien!"

The name passed through the Seric ranks. "Li-Jien! Li-Jien!" It reached the people outside the Great Wall. "Li-Jien! Li-Jien!" they shouted.

Cerdic repeated the name. "Why have they chosen that, do you think?"

"You can't guess?" Mago gave a grunt of amusement. He leaned on Hannibal's Leg. "It means—Rome! Li-Jien is the Seric name for Rome."

There was an expression of wonder on the Carthaginian's face. He turned his sightless eyes up to the sun. At the same time he put his arm affectionately round his nephew's shoulder.

"Li-Jien," he whispered. "Was there ever such news for an explorer to carry home? A Roman city beyond the North Wind."

End-note

One of history's most astonishing curiosities, the existence of an ancient Roman city on the borders of China has been accepted as a very real possibility since the idea was put forward by an American historian, Homer H. Dubs, in 1955. In a lecture delivered on November 23rd of that year, and published by the China Society (Sinological Series No. 5, edited by S. Howard Hansford), Mr Dubs argued that Roman soldiers fought for the Hun or Hsiung-nu war lord, Jzh-Jzh, against the forces of the Emperor of Heaven, in the autumn of 36 BC.

His evidence for this comes from surviving descriptions of a pictorial record the Chinese made of their successful overthrow of Jzh-Jzh. Indeed the fact that the Chinese made such a record seemed to indicate Roman influence. Until this time the Chinese, or Seres, had never immortalised their victories in this typically-Roman way.

A Chinese artist painted eight scenes on a roll of cloth, describing the attack upon Jzh-Jzh's capital on the Talass River. The double palisade around the city, faithfully portrayed, was a traditional Roman defence. There is no evidence that any other peoples in the middle or far east used it.

Yet even more convincing was the artist's depiction of the Roman Testudo, the "fishscale" formation of shields, which was a singular, and unique, hallmark of Roman defensive fighting.

It is possible, of course, that the Hsiung-nu copied Roman methods of defence and warfare, but the evidence of the Romans continues after the battle.

Mr Dubs refers to an Imperial Register of AD 5 in which the Chinese Emperor Wang-Mang renamed a western city. He called it Jie-Lu which, Mr Dubs says, can mean two things: "Caitiffs (Captured) in storming (a city)" or, simply, "Caitiffs raised up". The former name for this city was Li-Jien, the earliest Chinese name for Rome and its empire. It was pronounced with an "x" as in Alexandria (which perhaps the Chinese confused with Rome).

A settlement of Romans—to defend the western trade routes which Jzh-Jzh had severed—grew into a small city. The 145 Roman survivors intermarried. They would have had a centrally-appointed Chief or Magistrate, and their existence among the counties of China was listed until the fifth century AD. Possibly because of a population decline, the city lost status. It may have been destroyed in about 746 when Tibetans overran the whole area.

Mr Dubs believes that the "Caitiffs" were survivors of the 10,000 prisoners taken by the Parthians after Carrhae. Pliny, the Roman historian, recorded that the prisoners were marched 1,500 miles from Carrhae to Antioch in Margiana, some 450 miles from Jzh-Jzh's capital. No further reference is made to them.

Slender though Homer Dubs' monograph is, it opens a lost chapter in history. It can only be hoped that one day archaeologists digging in the ruins of an ancient villa on an island near the North African coast, will unearth the Log of Mago the

End-note

Carthaginian. They will probably find it in a casket wrought by Seric craftsmen, and wrapped in the same glistening material of which the Parthian banners were made: Widuhar's Golden Banners.

Today, we call it silk.

J. W.